Searching for the Light

Lucia Raynes

Searching for the Light

Library of Congress Control Number: 2014952586

ISBN 9780991481156

To my Aunt Helga who always has been a mom to me
more than my own mother,
she has been my greatest inspiration

Table of Contents

Chapter 1

Darkness, everything is cold and damp. Not again, I am thirsty and hungry too. Why is the floor so soft? I am crying for mom, banging on the locked door, why doesn't anybody open the door? My little three year old mind then realizes that I am locked in the basement, actually more like a dungeon. Locked away, for something bad I'm supposed to have done, by my devious, vindictive, Step Grandmother Rosa, and I begin to weep. Why is she doing this to me? What did I do this time? Why is my mom not here, where is she?

I wake up, one look at the alarm clock its 4:00 AM. My sheets are wet from sweating, another one of those dreams. I hate to wake up like this. I go in the kitchen to make some coffee. I can't go back asleep again anyway. I'm searching for the light. When are those dreams going to stop? Am I going to be insane in the near future, why do I have them after all those years? I pour myself a cup of coffee, light a cigarette, and think about my life, my screwed up life, like so many nights before. How far can you think back in your life?

Some people say they remember when they were born. I don't recall my birth, but I remember a lot of events, important events the kind that are stuck in your mind. My mother was twenty-four years old, when I was born. She was not married, which was unthinkable back in the early sixties. She grew up in a small town in Germany, with two brothers and two sisters. Her mother, Augusta, was a very strict, headstrong, ambitious woman. She was married to a bricklayer, who worked hard all his life in construction but she was never satisfied with their life. They rented an apartment from her wealthy best friend. Throughout the years, I guess Grandmother became jealous of her, because her friend had her own house and she didn't. After a while she started nagging Grandpa about building their own house. Uncle Fonsi, who followed in his Dad's footsteps, was already working as a bricklayer, building houses. Uncle Siggi was going to trade school to become a bricklayer too. They both had to help Grandpa, in building Grandma's house. The house was completed in 1959.

The whole family moved into this two story, nice, brand new place. Grandma started to charge her children rent. My mom was twenty two years old and single at the time. She worked at a sewing plant in our town, from the time she graduated high school. My oldest aunt had moved into the house, with her husband and two children. They were trying to save up to buy a house, but also had to pay their share. My oldest uncle had to pay rent to her, even though he helped build the house. The twins, my youngest aunt Christa, and Uncle Siggi, who was still attending trade school, had to pay their share. As long as Grandma could be the housewife and have her dream of her own house, even the expense of other people like her own children, she was happy. It may sound cruel, mean and intolerant but the more I found out about Grandma, the more bitter and unforgiving I became toward her. I believe she took more than they all could handle. My Grandpa started to butcher at night and on weekends, to bring in more money. He worked all the time, and the little free time he had, he spent at the club in town to have a couple of beers.

My mom was supposed to be the black sheep of the family, according to my Grandma, "She had her own stubborn, selfish, unpredictable mind". Eventually Mom tired of, as she described it later to me, the so called, "monotony of the sewing factory along with, coming home to deliver her paycheck to Grandma, without having a life." She took off to the "big city Frankfurt", to proceed with a career as a Restaurant and Hotel Associate. At the age of twenty three she started dating a nineteen year old boy, and became pregnant. Needless to say, she came back home. Years later, I found out that my dad had asked her to marry him, but she told him no. When I asked her later she told me, all she wanted was a baby, not a husband.

I was born in November 1960, another person added to live in Grandma's House. I was told My Grandpa was so ashamed and embarrassed because of me, that he would not touch me, hold me, or even come close to the crib in the first few weeks of my life. One day, My Grandma made him pick me up, I was told, and from then on I was his, "Favorite Grandbaby." It even got to the point, where he told everybody, that I was going to inherit the house, once him and grandma were gone.

Chapter 2

Well, life went on in the house, mom apparently was not happy. She went back to work at the sewing factory, and Grandma took over raising me. I guess, according to grandma's spending habits, money was still running short. Years later I found out, my Dad paid a very generous amount of child support, and mom, believe it or not, gave it to grandma, all eighteen years. I call it Mom's guilt money. I found out this money was being used for Grandma's house payment. My oldest, Uncle Fonsi would later often tell me, "You will inherit this house one day, because your Dad actually paid for it." Back then, I didn't understand what he meant by that. Grandpa's drinking habits didn't help either up to this day I believe Grandma drove him into drinking. He died in bed one night at sixty years old. He'd had a heart attack. I was two at the time, and I don't have any recollection of him.

After Grandpa died, Grandma enlisted her children in helping the richest and biggest farmer in town during harvest season, to help bring some more money in the household, since grandpa's income was gone. One of the three sons of the farmer's wife was still a bachelor. My Grandma, still embarrassed and ashamed of having a single daughter and her baby living in her house, and the farmer's wife, worried about her thirty four year old, still single son, then started to play matchmaker. They arranged a marriage between the two. I don't know if mom ever loved my Step Dad, or if she just wanted to get out of Grandma's house, but they got married. When I was two years old, Mom and I moved into the farmhouse to live with my Step Dad and his parents, and that's when I started remembering things.

My Step Grandmother apparently assumed that I would stay with my Grandma, when mom and her son got married. When we both moved in, she became ill-willed with my mom and me. I remember that I was in a "place" for a whole year, Mom and my Step Dad would come to visit every now and then, later I was told, it was a sanatorium, for people who suffered from tuberculosis. They had to put me in there, because my Grandpa suffered from it, and since I slept with my Grandparents, in the bed for years, they assumed I had it too. Since it is highly contagious, I had to be put in the "sanatorium" to get well. Later down the years, I had discovered, there was no record of me being diagnosed with tuberculosis. This is very suspicious. After a year, I came back home very much to the dislike of my Step Grandma, and that's when she started terrorizing me.

At a little over three years old, I remember playing with one of the little chicks they just hatched, and accidentally squeezed it too hard. It died, she got so furious that she grabbed a pitch fork and chased me relentlessly all over the back yard. Mom apparently heard the commotion, and put an end to it. I don't know what would have happened, if mom didn't stop her. We had a basement, no windows, no floors, just trampled down dirt; I still call it my dungeon. Every time, when that women decided, I'd done something wrong, she would lock me in there, if mom wasn't around I sometimes would spend what seemed to me like forever in there.

Fifty two years later, it still bothers me, nightmares like the one I just woke up from, claustrophobia, to a point, where I can't ride in elevators, and crowds are highly uncomfortable for me. My heart starts pounding. I break out in cold sweats, I start shaking convulsively. Violence was on a daily bases at the house.

I remember one day Mom and I were standing across from my Stepdad and his parents and all of them were yelling, screaming and shouting at one another. Then my Step Dad stepped forward and broke my Mom's pinky finger. I was a child. I didn't understand why my Mom was crying, that she was hurt, and why my Dad would hurt her.

When I was three years old Mom and Dad started having one child after another. We had the huge farm to take care of, Dad worked a three shift rotation at the nearby carpet factory, besides the farm and at nights and weekends he would butcher. We kids never got to see him much. Mom had a big load at the farm.

So at age four, I had to help with the babies. I was feeding changing diapers, and babysitting. I was about six, when I had my first accident. I remember, as if it was yesterday, I was sitting on the back seat of the tractor facing toward the back, dangling my legs, when my right leg got caught in between the wheel and the fender of the vehicle. I still can hear myself screaming. Thanks to my dad's quick reaction, I still have my foot. He stopped the tractor immediately got me off the vehicle, carried me to the car and to the hospital. I was in a cast for six weeks, missed school, which wasn't a big deal, because, they moved me up to second grade after a half a year anyway. I was an advanced student, even with all the work I had to do around the farm. At age seven, my parents thought, I was old enough to learn how to drive the tractor. When my classmates, went to the nearby swimming park, eating ice-cream, swimming and having a good time, I was in the fields with my parents working.

Chapter 3

As the years went by, things got even worse with violence in the household, mostly between my Mom and Dad, verbally and physically. I myself went back and forth between living at the farmhouse and my Mom's Mother's. Both places were very unpleasant for me, violence at my parent's and indescribably strict at Grandma's. Later on, I found out, that every time Mom and Dad and his parents had a dispute over me, they sent me to my Grandma ,and every time it had calmed down, I had to come back home. I became a nerd at school. I studied all the time, skipped yet another year up to the next grade. I loved to read. I buried my nose in books, and started writing poems and little stories. I made excellent grades in math and discovered my talent in drawing and in languages. All I had seen was work at school and work at home.

Mom would buy fabric on sale and sewed hideous outfits for me, while the other children got store bought clothes. When I asked about it the answer was we have to save money. The times I stayed at my Grandma's house, I listened to her stories about World War II, the depression, how she tried to pull her sister in the bunker during a bomb attack and all she got was her sister's arm; stories you don't tell a young kid, right? She always told me to be tough. Don't cry she said, "it shows weakness, you got to be tough." She knew how to sew and she taught me, starting with Barbie clothes. When I learned enough, I started to alter the clothes that my Mom made me, much to her disapproval. We got in arguments. One day, after another argument, I did what I had done so many times. I went to Grandma to complain. At this point, I hated confrontations, "yelling", and any kind of verbal or physical violence but I was eleven years old. I remember another run to Grandma, after fighting at Mom and Dad's house, after my complaints, Grandma simply said, "Don't worry, he is not your real Dad anyway." Wow, now I wanted to know more.

Mom was called up to Grandma's. I confronted her and I found out, that she never wanted me to know my real father, for reasons I much later found out and I didn't understand. Why she even thought she could keep it a secret from me I don't understand, because the whole town knew anyway. Mom and Grandma got into an argument, because Grandma spilled the beans. From that day on, I pestered my Mom until she finally gave me my Dad's address. I knew she had to have it. After all, he was still sending money, which I had never seen. When I asked Mom about it, she told me, she was saving it up for my education. After that day, Mom and I became more and more distant and I finally decided to move in with Grandma.

I wrote my first letter to my Dad, and yeah, he wrote back. We stayed almost two years in contact corresponding back and forth, until he suggested in one letter, that he would like to meet me. At age thirteen, I finally met him. We agreed on a day, to spend together, and I hopped on a train to the next town, where he drove to in his car. We spent a great day together. He picked me up at the train station, and from the very beginning we had a mutual bond. I spent the next summer at his place. He had a five star hotel-restaurant. I met his wife, Waltraut and my half-brother Michael, who I bonded with from day one. He was only a half a year older than me. Wow my dad must've been a real playboy in his younger years. Waltraut on the other hand, never did care too much for me. When I questioned my Dad about it he responded, "She never really wanted to meet me and never wanted Michael to find out either."

Meanwhile at home I became confused while living at my Grandma's house. Uncle Fonsi never married, and lived with her. Most of the time after work, he went to the guesthouse and got drunk. I hated when he came home wasted. He wanted me to do things back then that I thought strange. He wanted me to touch his private parts, and in return tried to touch me in an inappropriate way. One day he came home, drunk again, and raped me. It was an incredibly hurtful feeling. My own uncle did those awful things to me. I smelled the alcohol on him as he breathed on my face. When he let go of me, I fled to my bedroom and didn't understand anything anymore. Of course, I was too ashamed to tell anyone. I just kept quiet and went on. He owned the house by now and he kept telling me, that the house was going to belong to me one day when he was gone, because I paid for it. Years later, I understood what he meant, when I found out that mom had given all the child support money from my Dad to Grandma to pay the house payments, "Her guilt money", I call it.

Mom and my Step Dad started having more and more problems through the years. He became more her husband now, rather than his parents son, very much to the dislike of them. They argued more and more with Mom and Dad, and as a consequence, my Step Dad started to build a house on a piece of land we owned. We had plenty of property anyway. Once the house was finished, they ordered me to move back in with them. I found out later, it was all because of tax purposes. The more kids that lived in the household, the cheaper the payment was, on the tax portion of the mortgage. Yeah, this was a great reason, to move back home. Here we went again, Mom and Dad had a teenager on their hands, and quite frankly it added to their own marital problems. Yes, I knew he wasn't my Dad, so I rebelled, against him and against my Mom. I had lost all respect for her. My life was not going too good.

Chapter 4

At age fourteen and a half, I graduated high school early. I already knew how to speak three languages, finished a course in typing and stenography, and was ready for the world. I remember my teacher came to my home, begging my mom to let me go to college. I always wanted to become a nurse, or maybe a doctor, but mom brushed it off, she replied, that there was no money, and I would not need an education, because I was a girl. I would get married anyway. Wait a minute, what about the money for my education? What about the money Dad sent all those years? I was furious, after I questioned her she simply told me that it was gone. She arranged, for me to start trade school as a tailor, at the same sewing factory that she used to work in. I started, Monday through Friday, going either by train or the bus to the next town about eight miles away, to attend trade school. I asked her if she could talk to my Stepdad's brother, Oskar, who is a pharmacist to see, if I possibly could start at his pharmacy as an intern. Later she assured me that she spoke to him and he sadly replied, "the position was already filled." Years later I talked to him and the subject came up, only to find out that she never asked him. Why does she do this to me?

I met one of the kids on the bus, Dieter. I remembered him from school, he was in a different grade than me, back then, and a nerd just like me, and he became my friend. We started talking, joking and later held hands with a few little shy kisses. This was my first encounter of some warmth and tenderness. I was seeing that there really was something else out there other than constant violence. After about a half a year of puppy love, I came home one day and mother told me the devastating news. He was killed in a car crash by a drunk driver. My little, for a short time happy world, collapsed.

After Dieter, I dated two more guys. Rainer was going way too fast, he broke up with me when I didn't want to sleep with him.

Then there was Michael, he wanted more than one girlfriend at the same time. Then, I met Silvia, a neighbor's girl one night at the town's civic center where all the teens usually hung around. Someone had a little moped or something bigger. I learned how to ride bikes. We all went to the disco on them. Silvia was the opposite from me, I was the school nerd, and she was hot to trot, jumping from one boy's bed into another, and I thought, "Hey she is fun." I started to hang around with her a lot after Dieter's death, because I couldn't stand to be at the house, with Mom and Dad and my other siblings. I felt left out because, I knew, I had a different dad.

Silvia and I continued going out dancing and drinking at the local town's disco. I started smoking cigarettes and her dad had a little moped. He let us use it and we'd hang out together, any chance we had. Sometimes we would hang out with bikers. I learned how to ride the big bikes. Silvia was the youngest of three brothers and three sisters. One day, she introduced me to one of her brothers, David, nineteen years old. I was fifteen, and flattered, that he liked me so much. It seemed like besides my friend Silvia and him, no one on this earth cared for me. I was highly insecure, bashful and without any self-esteem at all. I started dating him much to the dislike of my parents because his family had a bad reputation in our small town. At this time, I didn't know that the whole clan were alcoholics, and known as a very disturbed, abusive, violent family.

David and Silvia's oldest brother, Werner, used to work as a roofer. He was disabled from an accident at work. He fell off the roof and knocked his skull open. He was on painkillers, but he would still consume a high quantity of beer. One night Silvia, David and I came home from a party. Werner and David both were drunk, it was winter, and the family had a wood burning stove going in the kitchen, the top scorching hot. David and Werner got into an argument. They started pushing each other until David slammed his brother's head on top of the stove and cracked his skull again. Werner, screaming in pain blood running in his eyes, pulled a pocketknife and rammed it in his brother's midriff, tearing not only his skin but his stomach as well. With blood everywhere all I could think of was, "this is worse than at home, they are actually killing each other." I ran downtown to the post office where we had the only telephone in town, called the police and the ambulance.

By the time I came back to the house, there were two ambulances in the driveway, doing emergency surgery on the guys. The rest of the family, were sitting around the table playing cards. When the police started questioning the family, I couldn't believe what I was hearing. According to them, they, where horse playing and everything that happened was an accident. After my statement (the truth) an officer took me aside and told me to keep it quiet. He said, that they don't like to mess with domestic disputes too much. If it would go to court, the family more likely would stick to their story and nobody would believe me anyway. I just had to let it go. After that night, I started to wonder, if there was no end to violence. Is this normal? I've seen bar fights at our towns disco a lot. Well I guess it is normal. All I knew was that I saved two lives that night, but nobody in David's family including him, appreciated it. Actually they were mad at me, for not sticking with their story.

One more year went by I distanced my friendship with Silvia. She became quite a little tramp, politely put. I didn't want to go anywhere anymore. It seemed wherever I went, some drunk, idiots who knew me, would call me a bastard, and didn't want to associate with me. I drew closer to David, I felt like he was all I had. Nobody else wanted me. I kept on sneaking him into my bedroom at night, and sneak him back out later. We fell asleep one night, and he tried to leave in the morning, but mom caught us in the hallway. He mumbled something about being sorry and it wasn't really a big deal because we were getting married anyway. Excuse me, getting married? Didn't somebody forget to ask me?

Chapter 5

Times were bad at the house, I started hanging around David's house more, despite the fighting going on, and after all it was normal, right? Mom and I grew even more distant, since I stayed away from home so much. I don't think she ever liked me too much anyway. I overheard her telling one of her friends one day, she always wanted a girl with blond hair and blue eyes, I have strawberry blond hair and brown eyes, and my middle sister Marina has dishwater blond hair and beautiful green eyes. My sister Glenda matches her dream to the tee. Up to this day that girl can't do anything wrong in mom's eyes. She actually can walk on water. She didn't even graduate from high school. She flunked. She didn't even pass her driver's license test. But according to mom, she was her, "smartest little girl, in the world." Give me a break, Mom's favoritism became more obvious, even with the two boys, until she was about forty one years old and she became pregnant with her sixth child. At age sixteen, I hated my mom, but at the same time I felt sorry for her, and tried to love her. I was very confused. I was very book smart but I don't think I had any common sense. In July of 1976, my baby brother was born without an esophagus. He had to stay the first year of his life at a special children's clinic, but we went to visit him every weekend. I was seventeen, when he came home, and our house became too small for all of us. Mom, just like Grandma, decided to charge me money to live there, since I was fifteen. I thought, why not pay that money someplace else and have my peace and quiet?

David and I decided to move in together. We got a little furnished place together much to the dislike of Mom. I don't know why she was angry, whether it was because I was gone and she actually missed me, or was it because she would have less money, without my "rent"? She also didn't like David too well and maybe she was afraid for me. Once David and I lived together, I realized how much alcohol he really was consuming. One night, we had a bonfire. It was when the seventy's polyester shirts where in fashion. All the guys got so senselessly drunk, Lucky, David's best friend, stumbled backwards into the fire. His polyester shirt immediately caught on fire, or more like, melted into his skin. With everybody too drunk to realize what's going on, I reached into the fire and pulled him out. Yeah, I saved another life. I still have the scars on my arms. It didn't take long, before David started showing his violent side. I didn't have the time one day, to wash the dishes. Hey, I was doing an eight hour a day shift, just like him. He got drunk, fussed about the dirty dishes, took one of the dirty coffee cups and smashed it on the kitchen table. He crushed the cups broken end into my face. Needless to say, I thought I had to find a good lie for the doctor the next day and an excuse for work. From then on, he would beat me on a regular basis. I don't remember how often this was. If I threatened to leave him, he replied that he would find me wherever I'd go and kill me. After what I'd seen between him and his brother years ago, I believed every word he said.

I was nineteen years old, and already sick and tired of my life. With no way out, I was scared. We went to a bar one night. I had become the designated driver a long time ago. Once when he got jealous, because I was talking to another guy, he pushed me down the stairs and I broke my leg. I spent, thirteen weeks at home on crutches. This was a lot of time to think about my hopeless situation.

One night, I took a whole bottle of sleeping pills just to put an end to everything. Fortunately there was not enough and I woke up late the next day. I was happy to still be alive and promised myself not to be this foolish ever again. Shortly after this, in February of 1979, I was driving to work. It had snowed and underneath was black ice. It was very slick. I just had my license for about a year. Somebody took my right of way and I slithered on the ice, ran over a sidewalk and into a seven foot fence. I cut right through it and turned the car over then landed seven feet down in a frozen field. I came out without a scratch, but the car was totaled. David made a big fuss over the car, but what about me? I felt worthless, no good, and stupid. My self-esteem had shrunk down to nothing. I did pay him back several months later. We bought a brand new Nissan-Datsun on payments of course. Like we needed another bill, we were already broke. David's drinking habits, became very expensive. I was angry; I got drunk that night at the bar then took the car and ran it into the side rails on purpose. I didn't care about the next day, I just got crazy.

As time went by, the relationship became more and more violent. I tried, to refuse to have sex with him. I didn't want to sleep with anybody who would beat me up again. That didn't stop him; he would just put a knife to my throat and rape me. Again, I just couldn't see any way out of this misery. During that time, believe it or not, my Step Dad and I started to talk more. I was beginning to believe, their fighting was more my Mom's fault, because all of a sudden, he seemed like a nice guy to me. I didn't tell him about the problems with David, but I think, he knew, what was going on.

Chapter 6

My friend, Silvia and I started to get closer again. She was already married, divorced, and had two children, by an American soldier. She was trying to make a buck as a waitress at a local nightclub. David and I started to hang out there; we met Alice the owner and her cute boyfriend Tommy. He started to show interest in me, even with my scarred up face from the coffee cup, we talked, and for some reason, I opened up to him about my miserable life with David. He suggested, I leave David and date him. I responded "What about Alice?" he laughed and told me that they were just using each other. She was just a call-girl and showed him off as her young boyfriend. He liked her spending money on him. The nightclub apparently was not her only source of income. She had a hand full of Sugar Daddies. Finally she went on a trip to Acapulco for four weeks with one of them. During that time my relationship with Tommy deepened. Silvia and I ran the club while Alice was gone and Tommy was there every night. I was not afraid to leave David anymore.

Guess who helped me move, my one and only Step Dad. I moved back home for four weeks and learned the real truth about Mom and Dad's marriage. Mom was just like her mom, nagging bitching, constantly complaining and never satisfied. Dad on the other hand was actually a very caring guy.

Tommy and I got an apartment together, and I thought life couldn't get better than this. He would cook for me, we'd go out to eat and to party all the time, and we traveled all over the world and went to rock concerts. I actually got to dance with Bruce Springsteen on stage in Frankfurt Germany to the song "Dancing in the Dark." Every weekend Tommy would bring me a big bouquet of red roses, my favorite. I thought that I was in heaven. He even promised me, that I would go back to school, once we got to the states. College, yeah that's what I always wanted. He was talking about me going to The States with him so that meant that he was very serious about our relationship

I actually grew closer to my siblings again; David had done his best through the years to keep me away from them. During that time, I found out what damage my mom done to my sister Glenda. She had raised her "favorite, baby girl", to be selfish, vain and cold hearted. Glenda broke up with her longtime boyfriend Jack, shortly after I started dating Tommy. She started dating an American guy as well. Joe was a very nice, kind man. One night, all of us siblings went to the club with our girlfriend and boyfriends. Jack happened to be there, he tried to talk to Glenda, but she told him to get lost. He went outside and took a syringe, stolen from his diabetic mom, filled it up with fuel out of the gas tank of his bike, and shot it straight into his vein in his arm. Luckily we all went outside for some air, and saw him in the bad condition he was in, and Glenda's new boyfriend Joe and I, rushed him to the emergency room just in time. This was yet another life saved. Glenda's only remark was" just let him die; he brought it on to himself" I thought, how cold-hearted can you be little sister? Glenda and Joe moved in together, but unlike my relationship with Tommy, theirs was rocky to begin with.

I remember one night Joe just came back from visiting his parents in the States. He brought some moonshine back. They got into a fight; he guzzled moonshine, and got seriously sick. Glenda, on the other hand told everybody (Deja vu) "just let him die he brought it on to himself." It was left up to my mom and me, to get him to the hospital. On another night, Tommy, Joe, Glenda and I went to a party. On the way home, Tommy drove his car and I rode with him. Joe drove his 1972 Camaro, which he cherished a lot. He was too drunk to drive, so he let Glenda drive. Not only was she drunk too, but on top of it she didn't even have a driver's license. We followed them, and then she lost control of the vehicle in a very sharp curve and ran in to a big open field with one electric post in it. She hit it and totaled the car. I thought, this was the end to the relationship, but I guess he was very much in love with her. They got married in November of 1984.

Shortly after, My Grandma had a stroke and it left her paralyzed on her left side. A month later, she had a second stroke, and after this one her mind was gone. She ended up bedridden from then on. The whole family had to rotate to take care of her. I hated it when it was my turn, don't get me wrong, I loved My Grandma, but I hated to see her in pain. She was at home, in a hospital bed and the times that she recognized me, she told me she would go to heaven soon and that I was her favorite grandchild, she wanted to take me with her. She squeezed my hand very hard every time and wouldn't let go. It would frighten me every time. She died in April of 1985, right after Tommy proposed to me and I was actually happy that she was gone. She was out of pain. My mom told me that I was coldhearted.

Chapter 7

In November 1985, Tommy got orders to go back to the States. He was to go to school in Virginia. He asked me to get married and come with him. Of course, I said yes. I was on cloud nine. We went to Denmark to get hitched. He left in March to go to school in Virginia for four months. I was to leave Germany in July after he was done with school. Joe, Glenda's husband, was sent to flight school in Alabama in March, Glenda also was to come to the States in July, and so what would be better, than to leave together? I quit at the sewing factory, where I had been employed since trade school, in March and went to Munich. My dad Harry ran a restaurant there with his second wife Maria. I learned that, he met her on one of his trips to the Philippines; he traveled there a lot because he had relatives there. My Grandpa was originally from the Philippines. I wanted to spend some time with Dad before I left for the States. I ended up helping him with the restaurant. I met a lot of rich guys who tried to make their moves on me. I was flattered, but I was married and looking forward to seeing my husband again soon. I came back in June to spend time with Mom and my other siblings before the big move to the States.

In July, Glenda then eighteen and I started to work as bar backs at the club "The End Station" Norman, the owner, a good friend of ours, was what you might call "a wannabe playboy" was glad that we helped him out. I knew he wanted more helping out from us, concerning his sexual needs. After closing the bar most nights we, including some guests and close friends, would go to his house to continue to party. One night at his house, Norbert and Glenda disappeared, I started looking for her. I wanted to go home because it was five o'clock in the morning. I started opening doors in the house and yes, finally found both of them in his bedroom having sex. I never seen my sister so furious and yeah, mean. I told her that she was a married women, her husband was locked up in flight school going through basics, while she was whoring around. I finally got her to come home with me; Norman refused to give us a ride. He was too drunk, too mad, because of his interrupted fun. I started out walking, only two miles to my mom's house, not too far, Glenda followed me, mumbling for a while, until out of the blue, she attacked me, from behind, started beating me, two girls in the road fighting at six am when normal people go to work, what a site. I found out, how furious, relentlessly mean, and totally out of control, my sister can become, especially after she has been drinking. A long time after this incident, I learned that through the years she had physically attacked every single member of our family.

Three weeks later, Fourth of July 1986, after my mom made me promise to take good care of "her baby girl." Yeah right! We flew from Frankfurt Germany to Atlanta International Airport. I helped Glenda, to find her connection flight to Alabama. This made me late for my plane to West Virginia. I was supposed to meet Tommy and his family at the airport. We had three weeks, vacation planned with his family, before we headed down South. I had to catch the next plane, got there in the middle of the night, worn out and tired, but still exited; everything new, a whole new world opened up to me. Tommy's parents liked me very much from the start. His sister and I on the other hand, clashed from the beginning.

Unfortunately, it never changed along the years. We spent three great weeks in, what they call Wild and Wonderful West Virginia, hopped in the brand new, Audi GT Coupe we brought from Germany, and headed to Alabama.

Chapter 8

I came from Germany around the end of July to this scorching heat? How was I going to survive this? We rented a small apartment for two weeks until we were supposed to move into post housing. It was a nice apartment complex with a pool where I spent most of my days. It was like a small vacation. Time was up too soon. We got a house on post, the furniture came, I began to decorate the house and sorted out the stuff, that got ruined during the three months in storage. It took me two weeks to get everything the way I wanted and I approached my husband about me going back to school. Bad news, I guess once we got back to the States, he realized that the dollar wasn't worth as much as it was in Germany, so to my surprise, he decided that I needed to go to work.

What was better to do than what I did back in Germany and know how to do best? Yeah, go apply at a sewing factory! I got a job there and from then on I worked, Monday through Friday, seven in the morning until four in the afternoon, sewing blouses. Sometimes I worked on weekends. Sometimes we would drive to the beach. It is only eighty miles from here.

After a couple of months, Glenda showed up at our doorstep, having problems with Joe. We took her in to stay with us. After all, I promised my mom to look after her. Tommy was buying her cigarettes and Bacardi, her favorite. She was only eighteen years old, too young to smoke and drink here in the States. I found out that it is very hard to live with her. She drinks like a fish, is very demanding and controlling, and on top of that, she was trying to make her move on my husband. Soon there was no more peace at home. She got drunk and argued with us, and I had enough and asked her, no ordered her, to leave. She moved back to Germany. Mother of course, blamed everything on me, because I didn't take care of her like I promised. Both of them didn't speak to me for a long time.

Then we received a phone call from West Virginia. Kathy, an old friend of Tommy from high school called and said, "Tommy you need to come home, your Dad is in jail." Oh no, what happened? He called his mom, she wouldn't say anything on the phone, so we got in the car and drove nine hundred miles, nonstop. As we got there, we were told that his father had sex with an eleven year old girl. She was the granddaughter of his wife's brother. This was not good news. My husband's Dad is a child molester. And the worse part about it, he didn't feel any guilt, and he didn't think there was anything wrong with it. He told us, "it is her fault, she seduced me". He got four month in prison and another four month in a psychiatric institution. What was wrong with the man? What was wrong with all men? First my uncle, now him, this can't be normal or is it? After that, finally everything went back to normal.

We went back to Alabama and started hanging out with our next door neighbors, both from the Netherlands. He was a Dutch Liaison Officer. She was a housewife. Some of our friends, who we knew from Germany, also were stationed at the same place we were. Someone bought a boat, and we started going with them to the nearby lake. Yeah, I learned how to drive a boat, how to kneeboard, jet ski and water ski. It was great. The weekends made up for the boring time at the sewing plant, until my husband invited the Dutch Neighbors to join us at the lake. Both of them, I do have to admit, were fun to be with, maybe a little too much fun. They had so much self-confidence, while I was still working on mine. Pretty soon, it seemed like my husband and I were spending all our time with them, whether at the lake, the beach, we would barbeque together and go to clubs together.

Chapter 9

One day Kenny called, one of our very good friends from Germany. He moved here to go to flight school and he was looking for a place to stay. Tommy suggested that he stay with us. We had a three bedroom place on post housing, big enough for all of us. So Kenny moved in.

The sewing plant I worked in closed down so I found a job, hanging wallpaper for a company. This was one of the few good things that came out of my relationship with David. He had taught me how to hang paper and paint. Tommy had to go to school for three months in Virginia and he took his beloved Audi; Oh, how he babied that car. We had bought an old Volkswagen rabbit for me to drive back and forth to work, nothing for a long distance. One morning Kenny read the newspaper, and said, "Look, A helicopter crashed at Fort Campbell and seventeen soldiers died." We talked to Tommy on the phone, and he replied, "I hope Joe wasn't one of them."

Joe, my Brother in Law, was stationed there for four months. Of course, bad news arrived; my middle sister called and informed me of my Brother in Laws death. He was only twenty-seven years old. She was going to Kentucky with Glenda, who had to look after his affairs. She suggested I come for moral support. Moral support! They had been separated for years. My thought was Glenda was back for all his money, well let's go and see. I knew my little rabbit wouldn't make it all the way up there. Kenny, said, "I'll take the rabbit, I'll drive it around here, and you take my car, stay as long as you want." I couldn't believe my ears; he had an Audi, just like Tommy and was as proud of it as Tommy was too, what a friend. My husband, to my surprise didn't want me to go. For the first time in my marriage, I realized what a control freak he really was. I went anyway, much to his dislike. I took Kenny's car, and spent time with my two sisters, both of whom I hadn't seen for two years. Marina my middle sister and I were always very close. Glenda didn't get everything she expected, I found out. Joe had sent the divorce papers to Germany. They had arrived two days after his death and of course my sister didn't sign them. Joe had changed his one hundred and fifty thousand dollar life insurance policy over to his parents. My sister got the furniture, the car and a seven hundred dollar a month Social Security payment until she would get remarried. Needless to say she wasn't very happy.

Chapter 10

Shortly after I came back, Tommy returned home from school. It was May 1988. We both had never wanted any children for different reasons. He admitted he was to selfish to share his money and my reason was, that there were already too many homeless, poor, starving, children in this world. If we were to change our minds, we could adopt one. Birth control didn't agree with me, so throughout our marriage, we were on the "counting the days, system". Long story short, three weeks after he came back from school, I found out I was pregnant.

Once I told him, he was very angry. While I was getting more and more used to the idea of having a baby, he grew more angry and distant. He accused me of cheating with Kenny while he was gone and that, it was his baby. Kenny of course, got upset with him and moved out. One morning, my husband, told me to get up and get in the car he had a surprise for me. We drove over one hour then stopped in front of an abortion clinic. He told me to get in there and take care of my problem and was furious when I refused. I'll never forget his words he turned around and told me "you are going to regret this for the rest of your life.". There were times that I did.

After that, He became a totally different person. He started calling me crater face ever chance he had. What was wrong with him? He met me with the scars on my face from the broken cup. Why is he doing this to me now? This continued as he abused me mentally, not physically. I haven't yet decided what is worse. He ignored me, my actions and my wishes. We'd still go out with our neighbors, now even more since they had designated me as driver. My pregnancy was not very happy. I hung wallpaper up to ten hours a day, until I was six months pregnant. When my boss finally told me I had to stop. It was no longer safe for me and my baby he said. My husband was furious, because I didn't bring any more money into the household. We argued more and more, he was still accusing me of cheating on him with Kenny, while he was in school. Where was this tender, caring, warmhearted man I met eight years ago?

Glenda, my sister came down from Kentucky, to spend some time with me, she was three months pregnant herself, by a German guy, but her pregnancy wasn't as easy as mine. I never had any of the typical symptoms, I gained only 19 pounds, and she on the other hand, had them all. When I was one week overdue, Tommy was on nightshift, and I started my contractions. I told her to turn the oven off and take the chicken out, so we could go to the hospital. She dropped and broke the glass dish when she took it out of the oven. There was glass and grease everywhere. Then she got sick and went to the bathroom, well she wasn't a big help, so she called Tommy while I was on my hands and knees with contractions, trying to clean up the mess, she had made. By the time we finally got to the hospital, we had another problem, they couldn't sedate me, the baby's cord was wrapped around the baby's neck and head three times, and she was already in the birth canal. After not even a half an hour labor, I gave birth to a beautiful girl, Shiloh. I always tell everybody she looks just like her dad. All the accusations about Kenny and I were gone that night when he saw the resemblance.

Chapter 11

I thought things would get better between us from then on, but boy was I wrong. Now I had to stay home with the baby so I could breastfeed, she was allergic to formula. Tommy was still treating me like a stranger. We had stopped having sex when I was six months pregnant, and we never resumed. Now on the weekends, Tommy and the couple next door went out. I was at home busy with the baby. After I left the hospital with her I lost a lot of weight. I weighed 98 pounds standing about 5'-6" and it didn't look like I was gaining weight anytime soon. I questioned my husband one night, why he didn't want to have sex with me. Why, was I so undesirable to him his answer was, "If you would look like Marion, the next door neighbor's wife, I might consider it". I was too skinny for him, "wow", he already had my self-esteem pushed so far in the ground, and I considered myself as completely worthless, ugly and undesirable. I felt so left alone, miserable, and worthless. I asked him "Why in the world did you marry me?" He replied, "Glenda told Joe, that you and she were going to be rich after our grandma dies" In other words, he married me because he thought I was rich. I never realized how money hungry he was until then. I lost all respect for him.

Then came yet another day and another secret I would find out. I went to look in our roll top desk, one day, for some papers, and found two annulments and two divorce-papers with Tommy's name on them. I knew about one marriage before me, but he never told me about the others. After I questioned him about it his excuse was, "Would you have married me, if you knew I was married four times before"? Well, he had a point there. I wouldn't. But my point was that he lied to me. One Sunday morning my neighbor across the street came over and asked me, "Are you stupid or just playing stupid"? I was completely clueless, when she told me that she caught my husband and Marion, the Dutch women next door, in front of our house, in our car having sex. Wow! He denied every bit of it. I did find out later, from different sources, that they went out to party and got her husband drunk. By around two in the morning, they got him home into bed and continued partying while I was up, half the night, breastfeeding our daughter . I felt so trapped. If I would have been in Germany, I would have left him but I was so alone here, I was scared to leave. There was no way out.

Chapter 12

When Shiloh was four months old, I started working at the Post Exchange store three days a week, because Tommy complained, that the money wasn't enough. He would bitch about me not getting enough hours at work but at the same time, he would gripe about having to babysit his own child. Go figure, I couldn't do anything right. I was running between work and home and back working at the store. Meanwhile my lovely husband continued his affair with Marion. He threatened me, not to say a word to anyone, about this, because authorities would kick us off post, so I shut up.

Well, all fun has an end. He got orders to Fairbanks Alaska in November 1989. I was excited and thought everything will get better, after we moved away from here. This was the wrong answer. He didn't want to go, his reason was, he couldn't stand being around me through the half a year of nights they have up there. Why did he despise me so much? After requesting another duty station, he got orders for an unaccompanied tour, for thirteen months, to El Salvador.

He asked me what I would like to do during this time, stay on post housing or move to West Virginia and live with his mom and dad. He wanted his Mom to have control over me, but I told him, "I am twenty-nine years old, nobody has control over me but me. I wasn't going to live next door to Marion, that floozy he had an affair with and I was not going to live with his parents. I was going to live with my family in Germany.

Chapter 13

Two weeks before Christmas 1989 we drove to his parents. I was in the Audi with my baby, he in a U-Haul truck with our cocker spaniel Sandy and the things we thought we needed the next year. He spent Christmas with us and shortly after he left I started making arrangements to go to Germany. Mom was going through a divorce with my step dad. They stayed in different bedrooms, there was no room for me at the house, but she told me that my, still unwed, Uncle Fonsi, who lived in the house by himself, since grandmas death, would let me, the baby and the dog stay as long as we wanted.

In March1990 my father-in-law Donald, took us to the airport. I was looking forward to spending a year back home with my family, hoping that things with Tommy would be back to normal after some time apart. I flew in late and Mom suggested we spend the night at Glenda's and move to my uncle's house the next morning. At six o clock in the morning, the next day, my sister's phone rings. My mom was on the phone crying. She told us the bad news. My uncle's neighbor found him in bed, dead. He had gotten hit in his stomach at work by a forklift, a while back. He didn't follow the doctor's orders, didn't take his medication to prevent an aneurism and died of exactly that.

The next days were filled with arrangements for his funeral then the funeral went by. I stayed with my sister in her small apartment with her six month old daughter, who was a constant screamer and with her Doberman. The dog continuously showed his teeth at my little baby girl. I told my sister, if that dog would bite her I would kill him. Even after she assured me it wasn't going to happen, I still felt very uncomfortable. Since Uncle Fonsi didn't make a testament, didn't have any children or wife, his belongings were automatically divided between his siblings. No one even mentioned that the house was supposed to be mine. My mom told me she was going to ask her brother and her two sisters, if I could stay at the house during the following year anyway, but apparently they told her no. Everybody wanted to sell and split the money. Much later, after questioning them, I found out mom never spoke to them about it.

Why did mom lie to me? Did she hate me that much? At times I believe she regrets that she had me and looked at me as her mistake that she made a long time ago. My siblings and I grew apart from mom. She meanwhile was divorced. We would gather together at times, rotating at each other's places, until we were at Glenda's house one night. She lived in a very old house, and we stayed up late. I had never believed in ghosts but around midnight, things started to fly around the room, voices appeared out of nowhere, and shadows appeared we were scared out of our minds. Wow, hey Glenda you live in a haunted house. All of us decided, not to tell anyone, because, we didn't want them to think we were nuts. Glenda moved back home the next day with her daughter and her dog. Yeah right, Mom didn't have room for me, but when my sister wanted to come back there was enough room. Go figure.

Chapter 14

Well I didn't have any choice but to go back to West Virginia. I remember my father and mother-in-law picked me up from the airport. We had gotten home very late at night. My sister in law, divorced and living at home had just gotten off the phone with Tommy. He was in the hospital in El Salvador. He had shot himself in his leg. Wow, what now? Will things ever get better? He was coming home on convalescent leave. Two days later, we picked him up at the airport. I was kind of exited, seeing him again, after three month but to my surprise, he was very cold, distant and yes, angry. My whole world fell apart.

There was nothing left between us. He was home for four weeks and it was nothing but constant bickering, fussing and fighting. Sex was out of the question and when he was getting ready to go back, we both knew that this was the end. Now what, where could I go? I didn't want to stay here, so is it back to Germany? Couldn't stay there either, there was no room for us last time I was there. Well, Tommy's parents knew without me telling them, that I wanted to go back to Alabama, the place that's been my home now, for the last five years and where my friends were.

I got on the phone and called my friend Helen a woman I use to work with at the sewing factory, until they closed down. We decided I would send one box of my belongings a day to her address, until I had just the amount left what fit in the Audi. Obviously, I was on my own here; no one who would help me drive a U-Haul truck eight hundred and eighty miles. My father-in-law and I talked, he understood my point, even so, he hated to see his grandbaby leave. One morning I packed up backseats and trunk filled up, car seat in the passenger side. Back then it wasn't against the law. My dog was in the floorboard. I drove all the way straight through, in twelve hours. I just wanted to get home.

I stayed with Helen, until I found a one bedroom furnished apartment to move in to. My furniture was still in storage. All I had

financially was four hundred dollars a month that came automatically out of Tommy's paycheck. He had it set up like that before he left
for El Salvador. It was not enough of course with me not working,
plus a baby to take care of. I met a girl; Angela at this apartment
complex just divorced herself. She was from Germany too. She
became one of my closest friends through the next years.

   Glenda and I talked a lot on the phone during this time. She
wanted to come back to the states again, and what better idea, for
both of us to move in together, so we thought.

Chapter 15

June 1990 I rented a three bedroom house picked her and her one year old daughter Jessica up at the airport and we started living together. We went to yard sales and purchased furniture, she got a car. Everything was going pretty good. After a month we got bored, and decided to go to a club. The next door neighbor's teenage girl babysat for us. We stayed out late, drank, danced and had a good time. Glenda left, before I did, I was just enjoying my, what I called newfound freedom. I ended up, going home with a guy John, who I spent most of the night with at the club. He worked there as a bouncer. After not having any kind of intimate relationship for twenty two months, I guess I just went crazy.

After coming home the next morning, my sister didn't asked any questions of course, for her, it was a normal thing to do. John called after two days and asked me if he could see me again. He seemed very nice and we started dating. I considered myself separated, especially, after my husband refused to send money for me and our child. He left us broke.

I needed my furniture out of storage, all my things were in it, including my baby's crib. He refused to get it out. Everything in storage, besides his stereo, was mine. I had it before we got married but his explanation was "the things in storage are in my name, and they belong to me now." I ended up writing a letter to his company commander, and had a power of attorney within a week, to get my things.

Tommy was furious. He started terrorizing me on the phone, threatened to take the baby, try to prove that I was an unfit mother. I asked him," why are you trying to take her, you never wanted her in the first place." His response was, "I still don't want her, but I want her for Laura." Laura, his sister couldn't have children. Wow, what kind of a man was he? I was in shock, I knew right then that my marriage was over.

My relationship with John became more serious. We didn't just go out together; he spent time with my daughter too. He introduced me to his parents. They were very nice people; his father was a retired officer from the army and his mother who liked me from day one.

Then Mom and my youngest brother Harold came to visit. Mom got sixty thousand dollars out of my uncle's estate so they came to visit us. I should say visited Glenda and her daughter, because the whole four weeks they stayed, I felt left out. Her attention was focused on my sister and her daughter Jessica. Mom did give me three thousand dollars from her inheritance and she said, "that is the least I can do since you didn't get the house".

After they went back home, things with Glenda got worse, I discovered, that she had a serious drinking problem, a gallon of Bacardi in two days is too much. One day she saw an ad in the paper, some psychic, Paul, who she contacted. She believed that her late husband was evil, and that he was haunting her ever since our experience at the house in Germany. Yeah right, "Are you going nuts now Glenda?" This Guy convinced her that her dead husband really was haunting her and told her he was able to change it but it required money ha-ha-ha. I told her, "Please don't pay him anything, it's a hoax." Of course my stubborn sister didn't listen, he took all of her savings and then she called Mom in Germany to send her thousands of dollars more. Mom made a mistake she sent cash in the mail, but the letter never arrived. My sister accused me of taking it, because I usually checked the mail. Up until this day she believes it.

Chapter 16

I started working part-time doing house cleaning for a company, while she babysat our girls. One day I came home from work and both girls were standing in their cribs screaming. I found Glenda, passed out in her bed with the Doberman, and the Bacardi bottle next to her. It dawned on me, my sister is an alcoholic. I found a day care for my daughter. I thought it was not safe for my child to be left with my sister. Shortly after that, Glenda told me she found another place, she couldn't live with me anymore. I was too strict, just like mom. She moved out, meanwhile, I was still struggling with money so I put an ad in the paper, to do housecleaning myself because I didn't make enough working for that company part time. I started out on my own. I had to work more to support me and my child. I stopped answering my husband's threatening phone calls, got a lawyer to handle my case and moved on.

Soon calls about work rolled in. I began working in private households, and after a few weeks I got a job at the local radio station cleaning the place three days a week. Soon I had a full schedule on my hands. Then John's mom called us. She invited us for diner and also wanted to talk to us. When we got there, she told us that John's ex-wife had called her. John's ex-wife lived in Canada with their three children, and told his Mom that she couldn't handle the youngest son, Jamie and his drug problems anymore. He was only eleven years old and she wanted him to live with his dad. The problem was, John was living with a friend of his, and he didn't have any room for Jamie. So we decided both of them would move in with me. John's mom paid me money for keeping her grandson. It all seemed to work out so, I thought.

Christmas that year, John bought his son a pellet gun a few days later I came home from work, two police cars in front of my house, Jamie and his friend Chris from next door, got high smoking pot. I had no idea where he got the drugs from. The boys climbed on the roof of the house with their pellet guns and started shooting at everything in sight, animals, houses, cars and yes even people. One neighbor got hit in the leg by a pellet and called the law. After this, Jamie got grounded, but he would sneak out of the house at night and come home at daylight the next day, until he got caught by his dad. John and I got into more and more arguments over him until Jamie decided, he wanted to go back to Canada. He was twelve now, it was his decision.

Chapter 17

Things went back to normal, until one day I got a call from the owners who I rented the house from. They wanted to move in there. I had two months to find another place. I had two cocker spaniels, I bought one for Shiloh, too, but it was very hard to find a place to rent with animals. I took the money from my mom used it as a down payment and bought a house. In December 1992 Shortly after my divorce was final, I got full custody and child support for Shiloh. I received a few more phone calls from my now ex. He tried to convince me to go back to Germany with him. He didn't want to pay child support for the next eighteen years. I didn't pay any more attention to him. I learned how to stick up for myself, how to take care of myself and Shiloh, and most important being self-confidant.

John and I had lived together for quite some time now. He was my ideal man good-looking not violent in any way he treated me like a queen. Everything seemed almost too perfect. He was a painter and he worked out of town a lot. I knew him and his friends were smoking some pot sometimes. But I told him as long as he doesn't bring anything home it was ok. The times he worked out of town, I spent my free time with my daughter. I enrolled her into dancing and softball, and I started hanging around with Angela the girl I met at the apartment complex where I once lived. We would go out to clubs dancing on the weekends.

After some time I noticed more and more behavior changes in John he started losing weight. He was having mood swings and he sometimes would stay awake all night and then sleep forever. He started talking about having threesomes with some of his friends, I told him off, and later I found out, they were dealing with drugs, and John wanted to use sex as a pay method. Then I caught him one day in the bath room, doing crystal meth, all the paraphernalia was laid out, he was high as a kite. I gave him an ultimatum, it's either me or the drugs. Guess what, he packed his things and left.

That was the end of it. In 1995, after being together with him for six years why did he choose drugs over me?

I had a huge Great Dane at the time and had a big doggy door in my backdoor for him. Several weeks after John left he got so high on whatever he took and broke into my house through the dog door. I was in bed and he came in the bedroom, as I started getting away from him he kept on pulling me back by my legs. I had a waterbed at the time and he kept on pulling my legs over the wood on the bed until I finally gave up. Then he raped me, but I didn't scream. I was too scared with Shiloh in the next bedroom. She could hear us or walk in on us and she was only seven years old! What would I tell her? It was John, she knew him, she liked him, and she didn't understand why he left. I didn't want her to see us. Then he threatened me "do not call the police or I will come after you" and I didn't. My legs were bruised from my knees to my ankles the next day, thank goodness it is winter, I thought, I can wear long pants. Well Linda, get on with your life.

Chapter 18

I had a German friend Eva, who I met back in 1992, at Walmart and started hanging around with her more. She was married and had a little girl Jessica my daughter's age and a little baby-boy. Her husband Daniel had left the army. He couldn't handle the stress anymore, so he said, and opened up a bait and tackle store in town. She worked from four am until noon at the Walmart bakery. She would go to the store after work and ended up, running it for the rest of the day until six. He would leave to go home and do some, "paperwork", but eventually Eva found out all he did was play computer games and watch TV. After closing the store, she'd come home and take care of the children, make diner, clean the house and feed the dogs. I didn't understand why she let him treat her that way but then of course, through the years I'd been divorced, I became what I think of as the most independent women ever.

I started hanging out with both of them and their friends. I found out soon, all they would do in their free time was drink beer and smoke pot. When I was a teenager, my sister and I found one of my friends down by the river hung by the neck, murdered because of drugs. Ever since then, I despised drugs; I just got through this breakup with John, because of drugs. Now here we go again, they tried to get me to smoke too, but I stuck with the drinking. Sometimes a bit too much, but everybody else was, so I thought, it's ok. They introduced me to a good friend and we started dating, soon I found out, that he was married, I broke up with him. I liked him a lot, but I was not about to destroy someone's marriage. I remembered how much it hurts when someone does this to you.

About every two years I traveled with my daughter back to Germany, to visit. My step dad paid every time for the plane tickets. When I asked him why he was doing this, after all I was not his daughter and Shilo was not his grandchild. He replied, "I want to make good, what those three women messed up" talking about his mom, my mom and my grandma, and he told me, "listen, you are my oldest child, and Shiloh is my firstborn grand-child, as simple as that." I know now, he was really a wonderful man. Eva's friend nick came to visit from Germany and I started dating him, we talked about getting married and my daughter and I moving back to Germany. Then, shortly after he went back home I flew to Germany to visit and found out who he really was nothing but an arrogant controlling selfish tyrant, who knew everything better. Well, needless to say, I broke up this relationship.

I was back to hanging with Eva and friends. Everybody seemed to get more and more crazy. Everybody slept with each other's spouse or girl and boyfriend. I knew, I had to get out of this. One night, we were sitting around drinking, when her husband started going into convulsions. Eva was too drunk to even realize what was going on so one of our friends and I got him to the hospital just in time to save his life. We found out, he was harmed in Iraq, but it was too late to apply for disability since he already left the military. They put him on medication, and he was not supposed to drink alcohol while on it, but he did anyway which affected his behavior. He became violent, and aggressive. My friendship with all of those people started falling apart; this was even too crazy for me. Eva kept on sleeping with her husband's best friend, he was sleeping with someone else, my married ex-boyfriend wanted me back, and everybody drinking and smoking pot like crazy. Daniel ran his store into bankruptcy. While Eva and the kids went to Germany, to visit family, he packed up his belongings, abandoned the house and moved back to New York where he was from. Eva called me one day to check and see, if he was still there. I found out that he left their dog, Cujo, on a three foot rope, no food, no water, for who knows how long. He was gone, I rescued the dog and found him a good home but not without reporting him to the authorities. I always have loved animals, especially dogs, I sometimes think I like them more than people.

Chapter 19

During the next few weeks, Angela and I got back in touch again, she is the type of person, who will neglect her friends while she is in a relationship but remembers her old friends when things get sour. She had met William whose parents were filthy rich, she told me, "I am going for the money this time like a lot of other girls." I told her that money does not make you happy. He was a drug addict, alcoholic, schizophrenic man. After they got married and had a little girl and got divorced, she contacted me again. I started hanging out with Angela we both where single again. She introduced me to Bobby, a friend of hers. He and I became instant friends and started spending a lot of time together. He told me he was attracted to me and wanted to date me but all I wanted right now was a friend. I wasn't attracted to him, I never liked big men and he was very much overweight.

Angela and I went out dancing one night, and that's when I met Will, my dream man, so I thought, very good looking, warm and caring. We spent that night together at my house, and the next day, I was on cloud nine. We seemed to be the perfect couple. He lived in the next town, had some property, including a beautiful lake. He owned the three trailers that were on it, he lived in one of them with his two roommates and he rented the others out to two young couples. After a short time of dating he proposed to me and I accepted. My daughter and I spent a lot of time at his place she got to ride the horse he owned, we loved it out there. He had big plans for us he wanted to build us a house by the lake and bring more trailers in to rent. I was going to sell or rent my house. I started, spending a lot of time out there, with my daughter. She got along with him and of course I liked that. I found out that the other two couples who rented from him were smoking pot. After I questioned him he replied, "I can't tell them what to do." I am just their landlord. I still didn't like the idea, that people would do drugs on the property, but I didn't say anything else.

One of my clients I was cleaning for, lived close by, and I was there cleaning one day. The weather was awful, it was storming and we had tornado warning after I was done cleaning his house lightning struck, and hit me as I tried to grab a hold of the door nob, threw me into the living room, and paralyzed my left arm. Later I found out, the owner had installed his own alarm system, the wire was wrapped around the front door, but it was defective, and lightening hit the door and struck me by grabbing the doorknob. I didn't know how long I was out, but when I came to all I wanted was to get out of the house. I couldn't use my arm at all. Driving, my five-speed would make it hard with one functioning arm to drive all the way home to my house, so decided, to go to Will's house. It was unexpected for him, and to my surprise, when I walked in the door there was a girl laying on his couch sleeping. He and his roommates were drinking whiskey. When I questioned him, he told me they went out to the nearby stripper bar and that she was one of the strippers. They brought her home with them and they all had fun with her all night. He was drunk, and I remembered my grand-ma used to say little children and drunks tell the truth. Then he told me since he was not married yet he could do whatever he wanted to. Well, that was the end of it. Once I got the feeling back in my arm, I packed the few things I had there and left. My mom told me one time, Linda you are my smartest kid out of all six, but when it comes to men you are completely stupid. Maybe she was right.

Chapter 20

The next year, I just worked and stayed busy with my daughter's activities, ball practice, ballgames, and slumber parties. Her friends always liked to come to my house, all the kids called me mom. One day a couple that I cleaned for, wanted to introduce me to one of their friends, just divorced and very lonely. We set up a date at a restaurant, and we clicked. Greg was employed at a nuclear plant and he seemed very interesting to me. He was a five degree black belt in martial arts, and soon I started going to his Dojo to train as well. He had a fourteen year old girl from his first marriage and a six year old boy from his second wife. He asked me, to marry him very soon, but I told him, that I needed some time. We had a lot of good times together. One summer my brother Siggi and his girlfriend came to visit and we had a great time. We went canoeing at the river, to waterparks, the beach and went to car races, it was great. The following summer, Siggi visited again this time with my brother-in-law Fred. Same thing, we showed them all over the place and we had the greatest time. Greg and I dated for three years. We trained together in our Dojo. I got a black belt in martial arts, yes, and we were pretty busy. In the meantime, I had to put up with his two ex-wives, who were still very much in his life. We even went to his daughter's softball games together with his first ex-wife, her husband, his second ex-wife and their son. Then his second wife decided she wanted him back, and tried her best to break us apart. He didn't want her back, on one hand he wanted to be with me. On the other hand there was his ex-wife, who had cheated on him, but she had his son and he adored him. I guess he had a hard time coping with it. He always drank a lot of beer, but it got to the point where he started on beer as soon as he woke up, until he went to bed. In February 2000 I had my daughter's birthday party at the house and the kids dared me to jump on the trampoline with them. I did, and landed wrong and broke my ankle on both sides. He was drunk, couldn't get me to the hospital until the next day. He had a trip planed with his friends to Costa Rica even though, I needed him, not able to walk, being on crutches, but he went on this trip anyway. I was disappointed. He wasn't there for me when I needed him. I thought, what makes me think he would be there for me in the future? I couldn't deal with the situation anymore, and broke up with him.

Here I was, not being able to drive Shiloh when she needed a ride to school. I was unable to work, what's next? I called my German friend, Marina, who I had met a while back at the veterinarian's office that I brought my dogs to. She was the receptionist there. She didn't hesitate to help me. She drove me and my daughter anywhere we needed to go, what a great friend. Then My Step Dad sends me money again to come home to visit. He told me, "You can't go to work anyway, what better time to visit?" Shiloh and I went back to Germany for three weeks. During my visit, Glenda told me one day, that she would like to come to visit, so I told her that she was welcome anytime to stay with me. After I got back home, I got off my crutches, and went back to work. I was single again, but that's what I wanted right now. Maybe my mom was right; maybe there was nobody out there for me. Maybe I did pick the wrong men.

I still had Angela who I went out with occasionally dancing and drinking. I had a few wild nights then, but why not, there had been nobody to answer to. I was footloose and fancy-free. I didn't need a sitter anymore. Shiloh was old enough to stay by herself. Then in October Glenda and her daughter came to visit for four weeks. My mom gave her a phone number of an old childhood friend of hers Elli. She told us to go and visit her. She lived only one hundred and fifty miles from me. Hello mom, how come you didn't give me that number before? I could've gotten in touch with her a long time ago. Why did she give it to Glenda? I swear I will never understand my mom. Well Glenda, me and our girls, got in the car and visited Elli and her boyfriend Dough. Elli never did like Glenda too much, but she became instant friends with me. We have stayed in contact ever since. Shiloh and I went to their wedding a year later, visited each other and even took a trip to Disney world together.

After we came back from our visit, I discovered that Glenda got worse than before. Not only drinking way too much but she had become a very vindictive, devious, manipulative, controlling person. She was trying to rule my household. I guess she was not happy with herself. She had put on a lot of weight and didn't have a boyfriend for a while. She was just miserable, and she was letting it out on other people. She tried to put a wedge between me and my friends, tried to order me around like she does a lot of people, but it didn't work on me. Here we were, constantly fighting again, until I finally told her to leave. I didn't take anything from anybody including my sister, yes I kicked her out. She left three days early and we haven't talked since.

Chapter 21

Two years went by, I was still single and soon realized, that I really wouldn't have the time for a relationship anyway. My daughter, a very sweet little girl from the day she was born, entered junior high. She got involved with some girls, who wanted her in their clique. She had to pass an initiation test. Well, I got a call from the principal one day he needed to talk to me. Shiloh's initiation test was to steal a pair of sneakers out of a girl's locker and wear them one day. Of course she got caught. The girl's parents didn't accept the shoes back after Shiloh wore them. They wanted one hundred and twenty dollars for a new pair. I couldn't afford that, so we agreed on me buying a new pair I managed to find the same shoes for sixty dollars on sale. Shiloh's punishment from me was she had to wear those shoes and no others for the rest of the year, every day rain or shine. Well, she started dating a boy, Chris, much to my dislike. I knew he was smoking pot. He'd been in juvenile detention several times. I was not very happy. My daughter on the other hand was infatuated by this boy. Her grades went down, and she stopped minding me. She became totally aggressive, disobedient, yes even violent. One night, she started packing and told me, his mom Liz told her, if she and I ever had any problems getting along, she could come and live with them. She even told her that she could share a room with Chris at her house. I told her that it was out of the question for her to leave and after arguing back and forth, she tried to hit me. I, on the other hand, picked up the phone and called the police. A female officer showed up and informed her that she needed to stay with me and obey my rules. She just couldn't pack up and move. After a few weeks of constant arguing and fighting, she tried to pack again. I tried to stop her and she ended up slamming my hand between the door and doorframe. Well, my hand was bleeding. I just went on the phone and called the law again. This time two male officers came and as soon as they walked in the door, my daughter started crying and talking about child abuse. The officers calmly informed her, that this situation looked more like parent abuse and that she looked very much unharmed. I on the other hand was the one that was bleeding. They threatened her that the next time they had to come here, they would pick her up and would place her in the nearby diversion center for one night. After they left, she told me "mom you will regret this." Wow she sounded just like her dad years ago. I let her date Chris; I figured she will find out herself that he is not the right guy for her.

Chapter 22

In the summer of 2004 my phone rings. Harry, my dad, was on the phone. He had moved to the Philippines at the same time I moved to the States. He called me from Germany and told me he had moved back home. He told me, that he went through three typhoons in the Philippines, and the last one that hit took everything he owned. He moved with his wife, and meanwhile three more children, my half siblings that I have never met, back to Germany. In 2003 his wife started cheating on him and they separated a few months after. He wanted to come and see me and his granddaughter whom he had never met. Wow, what a surprise, I hadn't seen my dad since 1986 when I left Germany. He told me he was going to get a plane ticket, at some time in December, and wanted to stay for three months. I was so excited about that, I wanted for him to get to know his granddaughter and was looking forward to spending some time with him.

In November I started decorating for Christmas, I wanted everything to be perfect when he got here. Shiloh and I were putting Christmas lights on the roof one day, but half of the lights that I saved from last year, weren't working anymore. I told her I was going to the store to get some more lights, and to stay off the roof while I was gone. When I came back she was still on the roof, and a man was helping her with the lights. That's when I met Tom. He was refinishing a floor at my next door neighbor's house, saw her on the roof then started to help her. He didn't want her to fall. Tom, fourteen years older than me, became a real good friend through the next few weeks. He wasn't my type, too old and walked funny from what he told me was back and foot injuries from when he was in Vietnam. Even though I was forty-four years old; I was still in very good shape. A lot of people thought I was around thirty. Right before Dad arrived, we started dating. I was at the point where I looked more for the inner qualities of a man then at the outside. I had enough bad experience with good looking guys.

We picked dad up from the Atlanta airport on the seventeenth of December. We came home sat together all night talking. We finally went to bed at four in the morning, but an hour later, I woke up again, because my neighbor knocked on our door, and yelled, "fire, Linda your house is on fire." I jumped out of bed, got Shiloh and dad up, got the dogs out of the house, and we evacuated. Well my neighbor was wrong. It was my next door neighbor's house that was burning down. Fire trucks and police and ambulance were there. What a morning, I assured the police after they questioned me that nobody was home. Luckily no one was hurt except the house burned to the ground. What a day for dad to start his vacation.

After a few days, I noticed, my sixty-three year old dad was in bad shape health wise. He was using breath inhalers, on account of his chronic bronchitis, and asthma, from his chain-smoking. I finally had quit smoking after my leg surgery in 2000 when my doctor strictly advised me to. It was a hard thing to do, after I had smoked twenty-three years of my life. We spent a wonderful Christmas and a great New Year's together. We went to the beach several times, my dad drank quite a bit of whiskey but I figured, let him enjoy it, he is on vacation. Before he left, it was the end of February, he got very drunk one night and told me a secret. I had a half-sister, Endai. He had adopted her from his wife's brother's girlfriend, who couldn't afford raising a baby. He confessed to me that he had sex with her when she was twelve years old. I was beside myself! I asked him why and his answer was, "It wasn't my fault, and she seduced me." Now Shiloh had two grandpas who were child molesters. I had already told her about her other grandpa years ago. I thought she had to know, after all, she went every summer for weeks to visit her grandparents. I wanted to make sure that he would leave her alone. Now my own dad, I was shocked, I was actually glad when he left, because I had lost a lot of respect for him. Shiloh had two perverted grandpas.

Chapter 23

Well life goes on. Shiloh who behaved fairly well while my dad was here, showed her mean little self again, after he was gone. One day she went to her boyfriend's house, his friend was there, he just got a brand new Mitsubishi Eclipse from his parents. I got a phone call from one of her friends. "Miss Linda, you need to come and pick up Shiloh, she is crying and bleeding." Oh my, what happened now. When I got there I found out what happened, all the kids where gathering around the car. Shilo was sitting on the back spoiler. Her friend told everybody that he was leaving, but my daughter apparently didn't hear him. She stayed on the car in the blind spot so he didn't see her there, while he was driving off very fast. My daughter flew off the car, several feet through the air and landed in the road. I rushed her to the emergency room, and four hours later, after they removed gravel out of her skin on her stomach, forearms hands knees and elbows, stitched up her forehead and put her broken wrist in a cast, we went home. I was supposed to pick up our plane tickets the next day to go to Germany but had to cancel the trip, because the doctor wouldn't let her fly because of her concussion. She healed up eventually, but she didn't slow down. I had put her on birth control at the age of thirteen. I figured I can't be around her 24/7 so I thought it was the best thing to do. I thought, she was safe while she was dating Chris, but she stopped the pill and became pregnant at age fifteen. When I asked her why, she told me, "Chris and I planned it, I told you, and you would regret it, not letting us move in together." She is supposed to start high school and she was practicing for color guard in band. I was at the end. I told her that she had the choice between move in with her dad or an abortion. I raised one baby by myself and I wasn't about to raise another one. The summer came to an end.

She started practice with the band. My neighbor's two girls, who were best friends with Shiloh, came back from Georgia, where they visited their dad every summer. They came over the first night, and

Amanda, the older one, and Chris, I guess fell in love. He broke up with my pregnant daughter, and started dating the other girl. He left Shiloh totally heartbroken. Even though, I was happy about the breakup, I felt so bad seeing my daughter so miserable. She was so stressed with band practice and the breakup. She ended up losing the baby. Meanwhile, I broke up with Tom, he became extremely clingy. I had enough stress with my daughter's situation, and I didn't want any man in my life right now. Life went on Shiloh got better in school, and started dating again. There was that one guy, Andrew who was among her friends whom I really liked a lot. I sometimes would ask her, "You are such good friends, why don't you date him"? She always replied, "Oh mom, we are just friends." Time went on, me single again, I liked it that way for right now. My daughter was doing well in school. I was very content with my life. I had it under control. I started teaching her how to drive a car and we got along pretty good for a while.

In February, 2005 when she got her drivers license, I bought her a used car, and she found a job as a waitress at a restaurant. After school, we actually had a great time, we got along pretty well. But good times don't last long. My daughter and her friend Ashley started running track at the nearby park every day after school. One day Shiloh came home and told me, mom I think you are going to be mad at me when I tell you this. Oh, let's hear this. She then told me that she got in a fight. I asked her if she started it and she told me no. I asked her "did you win?" She said "yes" and I told her it was ok. I had taught her a little bit of self-defense throughout the years and I also taught her not to start a fight, but to defend herself. The next day the mothers of the girls called me and wanted to press charges because my daughter beat them up. One of them had ended up with a black eye and a busted lip. The other one had a sprained wrist. I told them that there was nothing they could do, that we couldn't prove who started the fight.

I thought that was the end of it. So I didn't worry too much about it anymore. One day I get a call from the high school, the principal would like to see me in person. It was a legal matter so he had said. When I got there, Shiloh was in the office crying and the police were at the school. Boy oh boy, what happened this time? Well, apparently two girls who went to school with Shiloh, Liz and Heather, both hooked on cocaine, tried to befriend my daughter and Ashley, because they both had cars. They needed rides to do their drug business. My daughter and her friend refused to be friends with them, because they knew, they were doing drugs. So the other two ambushed the girls at the park one day, but ended up getting their butt beat by Shiloh. I guess I taught her well, Yay, self-defense.

The girls then threatened her, that they would bring their boyfriends to school to beat her up the next day. This left her scared. She didn't go to school the next day. Liz and Heather approached her the day after, with a fake doctors excuse already filled out, except her name and the date. They told her all she had to do, is give it to the principal and nobody including me, would find out about her skipping school. Days later they approached her again, told her, "Ok we did you a favor, now it's your turn." They needed a ride, so Shiloh drove them on their school lunch break to the bank where Heather took out some money with the debit card that she stole from her grandma.

Then she had to drive them to a house in the projects in town. She made my daughter wait in the car and went in to make a drug deal. When they arrived back at the school several police cars where already waiting for them. Unfortunately, for the girls the police already had the occupants of the drug house under suspicion and set up a stakeout, everything was on tape. I was furious. They drug tested the girls including my daughter right there on the spot and searched their lockers. Heather and Liz tested positive and they found paraphernalia in their lockers. Shiloh fortunately tested negative.

While the others were suspended from school, and had to face probation with the juvenile probation office. Myy daughter was put on supervision, which means she had to show up there whenever they would call and do a drug test. What do I have to face next, will it ever stop. I felt like I didn't really have a life anymore. I never liked to be alone, because I wasn't used to it, but right now I wished

I was. I threatened her that I would send her to her dad, but she begged me to let her stay here with me. I gave in and things did get better. I bought some drug tests myself and unexpectedly tested her but to my relief she always tested negative.

Chapter 24

Then another one of those bad phone calls. Dough called and told me that Elli had died, of a massive heart attack, at the age of sixty-eight. They were like my parents here in the states and like Shiloh's grandparents. Elli had suffered from fibromyalgia. They had some new medication for her, but her insurance wouldn't cover the whole amount of the cost she had to pay an extra six hundred dollars for it each month. Her son, Johnny was supposed to take care of her finances, but instead he embezzled every single penny of it. She was not able to buy the medicine. We went to her funeral, and I cannot describe how sad we were. She was such a good friend.

Back home, time went by and just when I thought those bad teenage years were over with. She dropped another bomb on me. In April, 2006 I had a rule at my house, Shiloh was not to have any people over especially boys when I was not home. One of my house cleaning clients had two children and I got along with those kids very well. The couple wanted to go out to eat on their anniversary so they asked me to baby sit them. After I got off that evening, I went home to change clothes and headed to my baby sitting job. At six o clock the couple promised me that they would be home by nine p.m. Well, they went out dancing after dinner, and they rolled in at one a.m.

I went home and once I arrived at my house, I couldn't believe my eyes. Years ago, I had turned my carport into a hangout for the kids. I put an old carpet down, an old couch and table and a swing, the perfect place for them. As I drove up there was a stereo sitting outside, blasting at maximum volume, a half empty gallon of tequila on the table, empty beer bottles and everybody except one boy was under age. I got out of my car and told everybody, "I am going in the house right now and take a shower, by the time I am back, I don't want to see any booze out here or everybody has to leave", and went in the house.

When I returned, the booze was still there and the kids weren't only still there, but they started playing cards. I got angry and told everyone to leave right now, and turned around to go back in the house. By the time I reached my bedroom, all the kids came storming in the house yelling "the cops are here, the cops are here". The neighbors must have called them because of the loud music, however since I was the first one to go back into the house the officers assumed that I was the first one that fled. They thought that I bought the alcohol for them and arrested me, for distributing alcohol to minors. I told Shiloh to call my friend Pat, who was a bails bond lady, to get me out of jail. After two and a half hours, which seemed forever, she got me out. I told my daughter, that she had to pay for this out of her own pocket. And later on, my lawyers costs too. Yes, I had to get an attorney, to get me out of this, even though I was innocent.

I started, like so many times, to wonder, what did I do wrong, where did I go wrong, what could I done better? I always wanted my daughter to have everything I couldn't have. Did I spoil her too much? I got depressed; I started to drink a little more than usual. I always would have two or three beers after work or some more when I went out on the weekends, but right now, I drowned my sorrows in alcohol. I felt alone, useless and worst of all, I felt like I failed as a mother. I started to resent my own daughter, and it seemed we grew further and further apart. Through the next year, until the following spring on the first of March, 2007 was a day, I will never forget as long as I live.

This was the most terrifying day of my life I guess. Shiloh went to school. I went to my first house cleaning job. After I was finished, I stopped by the house to eat lunch and then went to the next town for my next job. The weather was pretty bad, thunder, lightning and heavy rain. When I arrived at my destination, I turned the TV on; I did that a lot on my jobs, listening to it, while I was alone. After some time, the TV went off and the sirens came on. I still didn't think too much about it, I didn't see anything on TV all day about tornado or hurricane warnings. As I continued working, my cell phone rang with a number I did not know. My daughter was on the other line, calling from her friend's cell, repeatedly saying "mom the high school is gone, the high school is gone." I replied "are you ok, where are you?" She started crying and screaming. I had a hard time understanding her but finally found out that a tornado had destroyed the high school and she was in the underground shelter they just finished building at the church across the street, where they evacuated the children. Oh my god, I am starting to think, what was going on, what happened? I didn't understand any of this. The storm couldn't possibly be that bad. We lived one block away from the school, so I am thinking, if the high school is gone, what about my house?

Well I got in the car, and drove, no, raced to my house. I figured there is no police out there, trying to catch somebody speeding they, all have to be at the high school. I was right. The police were all over the area, blocked off every possible way into my street, I got as far as the church's parking lot. I couldn't believe my eyes. When I got out of my car, from the parking lot, two blocks downhill, I had a perfect view of my house, or should I say what was left of it. Not only my house, the whole road was in rubble and debris, everything totally destroyed. Electric cables were across the street with an awful stench in the air. People were running around totally confused, looking for their family, pets and belongings. It was devastating. I stood on top of the hill, I don't know for how long, thinking about all the years we lived here. My daughter grew up in this house, fifteen years. I had only five more years of house payments left, and now, everything gone, just gone.

My cell rang Manuela, my friend that I stayed in touch with ever since she helped me during the time I broke my leg, called, "Linda, get Shiloh and come to my house." I told her that I couldn't talk right now I was too overwhelmed and I hung up on her. Then, it dawned on me, who cares about the house, who cares about the things inside, I had four dogs and two cats in there, no doubt, they couldn't have survived it, or could they? I started running down the hill, jumped across the fallen trees across the road, the electric wires and all the other debris. As I got there, all the dogs stood right where the front door used to be, shaking disoriented, terrified, and happy to see me. What about the cats? I searched over and over but I couldn't find them, until one of my daughter's friends Jim, who didn't attend school that day approached me and told me I had to get out of the house, because there was a chance of the rest of the house could collapse on top of me.

Right, let's get out. I tided up my dogs on a tree, Jim and I went up the street again, running in every house, looking for people who needed to get themselves and their pets out of their houses. We finally got to the top of the hill, back at the church, the next thing, I said, "how about Shiloh?" I have to check on her. We went into the church, with high school children, thirteen hundred of them, screaming, yelling, crying. I finally found my daughter, thank God, she was alive, blood crusted on her forehead and one cheek, a center block had dropped on her forehead she had blood on her hand, but alive. She hugged me, crying, "Mom thank God you're alive." I took her down to the house to help me get the dogs to safety. As we finally got the dogs in my little Honda civic, a big challenge, a cocker spaniel, a beagle, a Chow and an almost two hundred pound Great Dane.

Manuela's husband Charles called, to tell me again to come over. I had to face the fact we were homeless. I unfortunately, due to all the stress, started smoking again after seven years. That night, while I was trying to get all the gravel out of my daughter's forehead, I noticed a change in her. She was scared. The next few days, she went through pure hell. One day she was crying all day the next was total silence. Night after night, she would have nightmares. I didn't know what to do anymore. I was confused myself but it passed after a while. This terrible storm took eight lives. After some time, we both got back to normal so I thought. I caught myself drinking more and more. I guess this was my way of dealing with the situation. We stayed ten days with Charles and Manuela. He started going with me to the house every day, all day long to save anything and everything we possibly could. She would come home after work and would cook for us. We found the cats the next day they were hiding under the rubble, too scared to move, but we were happy to see them alive.

Chapter 25

About three days after the storm, Charles and I were working at the house, loading up some of the things we could save, when Tom, my boyfriend back from 2004 showed up. He asked if we needed any help, and I nodded, I told him that we didn't have a place to go I couldn't expect my friends to let us stay there for too much longer. They were remodeling at the time and we lived in tight quarters. Tom said, "No problem, I got an empty house, I use it for storage for paint, and paint equipment. I will get it cleaned up and you can stay as long as you want."

My insurance had a place ready for us to stay, but they wouldn't allow any dogs or cats, so needless to say I didn't have a choice. I wouldn't dare part with our animals. We had rented a storage unit where we moved everything we could salvage from the house. Then we moved in Tom's house with our animals. I got my money from the insurance. All of a sudden, I had about two hundred thousand dollars in my bank account and a lot of work on my hands.

My daughter was a senior in high school, we had to get a prom dress, had to make arrangements for her graduation and get her pictures done. I had the rest of my house bulldozed down, and checked with construction companies about rebuilding it. With about five hundred houses in town destroyed in the storm, everybody told me that it could be a year before they could even get started on it. I was grateful that Tom let us stay at his place, but it was not really too livable, after all, he used it as storage.

I invited Shiloh's dad, his family and a lot of friends, her friends and mine, including Dough, to her graduation. I wanted everything to be perfect on her big day. I started looking for a house to buy. I was not the only one. All the other storm victims, who didn't want to rebuild, were out there looking too. At this time it felt like, somebody could paint a pig pen and sell it. While we lived at Tom's place, he and I started dating again. I guess, that was his whole plan, when he offered me to stay at his place. I don't know why I agreed to being together again. Maybe I was so thankful to him for helping me out or I was tired of being by myself. I was lonely and I wanted a life again besides raising a terrible teenager, but to my surprise, there was nothing terrible about Shiloh anymore. I couldn't believe how great we were getting along. She changed so much after the storm.

One day, I was walking with two of my dogs, when I spotted a vacant house, three houses away from where we lived. I didn't see a "For Sale" sign, so I left a note with my phone number on the door. Nancy, the owner of the house called a few days later. She told me, her mother-in-law use to live there. She passed away, and Nancy was getting ready to have an estate sale and then put the house on the market. After I told her about my situation, she told me to go inside and look at everything, let her know, what I could use and she would just give it to me. What a nice woman. I looked at it, three bedroom one bath perfect. I bought it in May, just three weeks before my daughter's graduation. Of course, it cost more than my old house, I bought fifteen years ago. I paid cash for half of it and financed the other half. We had everything ready and moved in just a couple of days before Shiloh's big day. Her graduation went well, and on top of it, me and her got along again. I think being in the storm and facing a disaster that close, completely changed her.

Chapter 26

In June, I decided it would be best to take a vacation for a while, so we took off to go to Germany to visit everybody for three weeks. I ended up spending a lot of time with my brother-in-law's best friend. By the end of our visit, he wanted me to go back to the states, pack my things and come back to Germany to live with him.

When I got back, and thought about it for some time, I decided to stay here. I wanted to go back but I just couldn't leave my daughter. Time went on and then the boy she dated, lost his job, and I allowed him to move in with us. Now we had a problem. The place became too small. I looked around and got estimates for an addition to the house, but everything got so high after the storm. Tom told me one day, "I can do it", and I asked him if he was sure, after all, he was not in construction. He was a painter. But, he assured me he was capable of doing the job, and a lot cheaper than any of the other companies. Unfortunately he was wrong, after several month of him working on the house and more mistakes piling up I told him to stop. He became angry about it, and again I terminated our relationship.

I finally found two men who knew what they were doing. They actually had to tear down some of the work tom had done, in order to get it right. My whole addition cost me more than what I had expected. I had to support me, Shiloh, who was at the time out of a job too, and her unemployed boyfriend.

I started losing clients. A lot of people I cleaned house for were senior citizens who died, or were put in the nursing homes by their families. My savings shrunk month after month. Plus on top of it, I was drinking more and I started on hard liquor. My friend, Manuela told me years later, that she thought the storm had pushed me over the edge.

In 2008 the work was finally finished on the house. I had a second bathroom and a sunroom added. My daughter and her boyfriend broke up, and she went to college. Between the two of us and both not having a boyfriend, we became very close. We were more like really good friends. One day I ran into George, a friend of mine. His wife had died a while back, and he and I started dating. I was reluctant at first because he is twenty-two years older than me, but he was wealthy. I was at the point where I thought, I am going for the money, like everybody else.

He ran a bakery and he hired me to work there to replace my lost work. I had to get up at three in the morning worked at the bakery from four am until two pm, and cleaned a house or two in the afternoon and then offices at night. Some days I put in up to sixteen hours, I was stressed and started losing weight by summer. I was officially engaged to my boss. I was reluctant at first, because of the age difference, but I had to think about my future too. In some way, I liked to be engaged to him, we would go out a lot, go to the beach and scuba dive. He had a little two seated airplane and he actually taught me how to fly it. But, our engagement didn't last long. He hired a young new accountant, and it was very obvious that he had the hots for her. As he worked me more and more, he would spend a lot of time in the office with her. My co-workers made fun of me behind my back until one of them asked me, "Why are you letting him treat you this way, the whole crew is laughing about you."

I caught myself having a couple of drinks before work and then during work. I believed I couldn't function otherwise. I started to wonder, what is it, about me, why do men threat me this way, cheating or want to cheat or physically and mentally abusing me? I quit my job at the bakery, threw his ring in front of him and left. My daughter was relieved she never did like him anyway.

Chapter 27

It was back to just the two of us again. In spring 2009, Shiloh got her degree as a surgical assistant. One night, she came home from a party, and asked me, "Mom do you remember Andrew"? Well, of course I remembered him. I always wanted her to date him. She said, "Guess what, we are officially dating." Wow, nothing could've made me happier than that. At least her life worked out.

Now back to mine. All I did the next month was work and stay at the house, Shiloh found a job at the local nursing home and in her free time she spends a lot of time with Andrew. After they dated for a while she moved in with him   I missed her a lot and felt very lonely. I missed her and I tried to drown my loneliness in alcohol. I went to bed with a drink and got up with a drink. It came to the point where I hated the smell and the taste of it, but I had to have it to function. I went to work loaded, came home loaded and went to bed loaded. I started shaking when I didn't have a certain amount of it in me. Deep down I knew I was on my way to becoming an alcoholic, or was I already one? Angela came by one day. She must be single again, I thought, because whenever she was involved with someone I would never see her. She told me she was on this dating site online. We went on my P.C. and started my profile on it too.

Soon, I chatted with several guys, met with two, but it didn't work out until the third one I got in touch with, Kevin. There was something interesting about him when we chatted. After almost three months, we decided to meet. He was on disability from a head-injury five years ago, but he seemed pretty normal to me. He came to my house, and we hit it off right away. The next few months, we spent a lot of time together, until I got a call from Germany. My dad had to have emergency surgery and wasn't doing too good. He is only sixty-nine years old. Please God, let him be ok! Another call, Daddy was doing better. After the good news Ken and I decided to get married.

Then, two days after our trip to the courthouse another call from home, dad had another operation, which left him in a coma. Within a week I had four more calls, my step dad, who has been on kidney dialyses for some time was in the emergency room with blood poisoning, his nurse messed up his port, my mom was in the ER with serious heart problems, my brother stepped on a rusty piece of metal, he was in the ER with blood poisoning and my niece who just had a baby suffered from postpartum depression and tried to commit suicide. She was in the ER too. Then the final call, my daddy never came out of his coma, he passed away two weeks after I got married.

This was too much for me. I was already hooked on the bottle, I drowned my pain. After living with Kevin, I realized that he was drinking even more than I did. I hoped, with him by my side, that I could stop or slow down, but there was no chance. I lost client after client because I wouldn't get up in time in the morning, to go to work. Then finally, Christmas Eve, after he had way too much to drink, Ken went in a rage over nothing, and started vigorously beating on me. Oh no, the same thing happened here, just like back in Germany with David, but this time I fought back. With what I learned in my self-defense, I beat him off me and told him to get out before I called the police.

When I was alone my whole world seemed to crumble in front of me. I went to the store, and bought three five liter boxes of wine and decided to commit suicide, yeah I'd drink myself to death, I thought. I couldn't see clearly anymore. Shiloh told me later that her and Andrew came by to visit and found me passed out on the living room floor, and rushed me to the hospital. The next thing I remember I heard the doctor telling her, that I had five times as much alcohol in my blood than the legal limit. And if they would have found me two days later I wouldn't survived. After that, there was darkness, bad dreams, hallucinations. I was in intensive care for two weeks, they were detoxing my body. Later I found out, my daughter was worried so much she and Andrew didn't leave me at any time during those two weeks. She slept with me in my bed and they put an extra bed in there for Andrew.

My daughter told me later that during this time I repeatedly told everybody that I didn't want to live anymore, that I wanted to die. Well, they put me in a, what I called it, "a looney bin". I don't remember the first weeks I was there, but the time I do remember was a living hell. The medication they put me on done the job, my body didn't crave any alcohol anymore and I stopped shaking but I was surrounded by lunatics. Some girls wanted to start fistfights with me, some going crazy trying to jump out of the windows, they didn't even realized that there were bars on them. It was torture for me being locked up, because I am highly claustrophobic. I spent the weeks that I do remember, reading, writing and doing math problems.

Finally, I was released! A local police officer picked me up, and drove me back to my hometown. He was a friend of mine, he told me, that he was a lot happier to see me on this trip than on the last one. The sanatorium was three hours away from home. I had to show up at the courthouse and sign some paperwork. And according to doctors' orders, I had to start seeing a counselor. My daughter came to pick me up, and told me that she had given my beloved German shepherd Lola away. This feeling was almost unbearable. I started cussing at her, yelling and screaming. All I wanted was to die again. I threatened she had better find my dog again, or else. I still had my other two dogs and two cats left at home but I was determined to get Lola back. Luckily the new owners got in touch with my daughter and gave the dog back. They told her they couldn't handle her. Apparently she seemed to suffer from separation anxiety.

Chapter 28

Well I was back at home, no job, no money left in the bank. Kevin ran me into bankruptcy, or, should I say we both did. I was happy to be back. After I spent four long weeks in that awful place, now I had to go on with my life. Then, my step dad called out of the blue, and asked me if I needed some money. Shiloh had called Germany and told my family about my situation and my Dad was trying to help me again. I think he was the only one of my family or my friends, who didn't judge me, who didn't call me an alcoholic. He sent me six thousand dollars to get started again. Boy, what a man, how could I have ever been so wrong about him?

Then, my husband, who did not call or visit me once in the clinic, called me out of the blue and told me how sorry he was. I took him back, and things where looking good for us. I found a job working graveyard shift at a nearby gas station, and he was playing housewife during the day. He would cook for me and clean the house. It all seemed perfect. He had promised not to drink anymore, and I believed him.

We were doing well, so I thought, but of course, it didn't last long, he started to drink again after some time and worse of all, he seduced me to start again too. That's when I started to hate him. I never hated anybody, before. I just let him stay because I thought I needed him to help pay the bills, but soon I had figured out, that most of his money went for cigarettes and beer. There is not much money left when you smoke four packs of cigarettes and drink a case of beer a day. We couldn't pay the bills anymore. We started fighting over it, and one night he beat me up again. I had a broken finger, broken glasses, and a very badly torn up face. He had grabbed me by my hair and kept on slamming my face on the hardwood floor. I managed to get away from him, locked myself in the bedroom and called the police. He got locked up for one night, and the next day he broke into the house. He broke my front door, destroyed my TV with an ax and started beating me again. He threatened that if I would fight back, he would tell them about my martial art knowledge, and then they would put me in jail for beating him up.

Sometimes I came home from work in the morning, and he would lay drunk. He had his pants half down in front of the toilet, and I would end up pulling his pants up and helping him to bed. I began to realize, that apparently his head injury did some damage to his brain. Nobody in his right state of mind would treat another human being this way.

I don't know why I kept on taking him back, maybe fear, fear of being alone again, or was it fears of not making it on my own. I believe now, that I was still in some stage of denial. What happened to this once so independent women I use to be? He would not only drink and smoke his social security check away, but he would take off to go to the casino and gamble away the money that was meant to pay bills with.

Then His nephew came to visit from Memphis Tennessee one morning. When I got off work, I found both of them sitting on the couch smoking pot. Please not drugs too. We decided to take his nephew out to town one night, they got drunk, and when we came home Kevin beat me up again. His nephew was so drunk he went to bed and didn't even realize what was going on. I called the police again but they had been at the house so many times they wouldn't even bother to lock him up anymore. The next day I kicked him out again and then sent his nephew back home.

A few weeks later, the next shock was, I found out that I was pregnant, at the age of fifty, wow, not good. Well, I had to call and tell him and he moved back. He was all excited about it. Then the electricity got cut off. We couldn't pay the bill. He rented a u-haul truck one day and told me that we needed to pack and leave. He had rented a trailer for us because we would lose the house anyway. I asked what about the animals and he replied that they had to stay back in the house, because the new place didn't allow any pets, and that eventually, after being abandoned they would die anyway. Oh boy, no way. I told him that I wouldn't leave the animals, so he got drunk, and told me that he would leave alone and got in the truck. I went after him because I didn't want him to drive drunk and he actually tried to run me over with the truck, on purpose. I fell down, and barely got out of his way. I lost the baby, looking back at it; I think it was a blessing.

Chapter 29

Now what? March 2011was here and I had no heat, no hot water, and no electricity at all and no money. Kevin had made me quit my job at the gas station back in November. I guess he was jealous he wanted me to be at home at all times. I had been so independent for so many years. How could he possibly change me back into this person that I never wanted to be again? The only good news I had was Shiloh and Andrew went to the courthouse and got married. I was so happy for them both.

Then one day I got a phone call from one of my old clients. His wife had passed away and he, nearly eighty, needed someone to clean and cook for him and drive him since he had cataracts. I moved in with him, the important thing for me was, that I was able to bring my animals. It seemed the right thing to do at first, but I soon found out otherwise. I had to live in a roach infested disaster. He couldn't pay me what he promised, because he had a son, who was a drug addict and he had to support him financially. His dogs started to fight with my dogs, and on top of it, the dirty old man took Viagra and thought sexual favors were included. He took in another girl Lynn, and started showering her with gifts and paid every single one of her bills while I was doing all the work and didn't get paid a penny. I will never understand men. He was an alcoholic, and would invite his friends to drinking parties knowing I was having a hard time sustaining the temptation.

I already started shaking again if I didn't drink every day. I knew I had to get out of there. It was just the opposite this time. I didn't want to die anymore. I wanted to live and live healthy not having to depend on any alcohol. I wanted to be in control again I didn't want to be controlled. I went out to Kevin's mom's house one night, to see, what we possibly could do about the situation, after all we were still married. His brother Harold was there a very religious man, yeah right. When I got there he cussed me out called me a whore, slut, bitch and a liar then kicked me out of the house and threatened to put a restraining order on me. This was very religious behavior all right. I did get a letter after some time to show up at court. I didn't go there sober, I needed alcohol to function. The judge listened to both of our stories and advised me to put a lifetime restraining order on him too. Yes, I agreed. As I got back, I got on the phone and talked to Reggie, my counselor. I had been seeing him once a month ever since I got out of the sanatorium and asked for help. He sent me to a psychiatrist who prescribed me some detoxify medication, and between that and my willpower, I finally broke loose from any alcohol.

Chapter 30

I finally moved back into my house in May. It was warm enough to stay without heat. Then I had to put my car in the garage one day and when they called me to pick it up I couldn't find a ride. I had no money for a cab, so I started walking to the garage, only two miles. As I started out walking, a pickup truck stopped and the driver asked me if he could give me a ride. I accepted, and we picked up my car. He followed me back home to make sure, I was ok and when he asked why I was without power I told him. He told me then, that he owns a few trailer parks and he had an empty camper where I could stay for a while but no animals. He also wanted me to work for him. All right, finally a job again.

I started in June working for him every day from six am until noon. We were cutting trees, tearing down old decks and building new ones. This was very hard work for a woman. Then I would go and spend the rest of the day with my dogs. When it got dark, I went back to the camper to spend the night. It was hard work. I learned how to use a chainsaw, cutting trees down. During my free time, I also put in job applications all over town. I had filled out sixty applications in four weeks with no response. William, the man I worked for, told me that he was running out of work for me soon and he also sold his camper.

I thought about Bobby, my buddy. He quit at Wal-Mart a while back and called himself an entrepreneur. He was doing scrap metal, with other words rummaging through peoples garbage. He lends me one hundred and fifty dollars to pay some bills, and then I started helping him. We went out every night, looking through peoples' garbage, to see what we could use. We picked up stuff good enough to bring to the next Saturday flea market to sell and worked the scrap metal as well. I never thought in my whole life that I would ever have to go through peoples' trash to make a living. During the day, I would fill out applications everyplace I could think of, hotels, department stores, restaurants, gas stations and fast-food restaurants. During this time Bobby made sexual advances at me. I had the hardest time fighting him off. I always thought of him as a friend. He is a very large man, and I never did like fat men. Besides that, I have been to his house. He is one of the most unorganized, dirtiest and sloppiest people I have ever met. I was not interested at all.

On Saturdays, we would set up at the flea market. Then one day a man, his name was Richard, came by looking at my CD's I had for sale. After he bought a couple of them, he asked me if I wanted to pack up my things at the flea market and come to the lake with him on his boat. It sounded great! When was the last time I've been on a boat, or went water skiing? But I had to make some money I had to buy dog food and pay bills so I told him no. He said, "Well what about going to the movies with me tonight, I'll pick you up." I thought about it, after last night and Bobby's clumsy, relentless attempts again, to go to bed with him, I told Richard yes.

He did come and pick me up that night. He was wondering why I lived without electricity. After I explained to him why, he told me if I wanted to, I could stay at his house in the guestroom, spend the night and I thought, hey he is a really nice guy. After the drive-in movies, where we oddly went with his daughter, her girlfriend and his grandson Kevin, we went to his house and spent the rest of the night talking. He seemed like he was a very caring man. We went out on his boat the next morning, rode the jet-ski and had a blast on the water. It was great. I felt like I was beginning a whole new chapter of my life! I met his son at the lake and discovered that I knew him. He used to date my daughter back in 2007. What a small world. The next day, I got a phone call from the military post for an interview, at the exchange store. This was the one I used to work for back when my daughter was a baby. I had put an application in not too long ago. I went there, got the job and things seemed to look good again.

I broke up my friendship with Bobby, because, he refused to pay me for the two months I'd helped him. I knew him; we'd been friends for a long time. He was very stingy, a miser. He called himself, "thrifty", but I never thought he would cheat me out of money I worked so hard for. I was supposed to be his friend. Looking back, I believe he was jealous of Richard, and that he resented me for not dating him.

Chapter 31

I started dating Richard. He lived in a town, about seventeen miles from me. His daughter, her son and his son Hubert lived with him. It was the family that I never had and I felt comfortable there. His children liked me from day one. It felt great! Although, I did have to get used to the totally neglected, disorganized house they lived in. I have a small case of obsessive compulsive disorder. I just call it overly neat. Every time I went over to his house, I would cook and clean for everybody. After all, I started doing my laundry there since I still didn't have my power turned on. So I felt, I should do something for them in return. I was still saving up for my electric bill. I needed to come up with twelve hundred dollars, including the reconnection fee. After we dated for a while, Richard told me that his daughter was lesbian. Her son Kevin, was a product of her trying to be with a man once. I fell in love with this little boy and vice versa.

Christmas came and he proposed to me, I accepted, we set the wedding day for some time in August. Within the next few months, I found out some disturbing news. I thought, I'd seen a lot in my lifetime, but I guess you always live and learn. Richard's mother was lesbian too. I met a lot of girls at his house, his daughter Cindy's friends, most of them also gay. He had a lock on his bedroom closet. One day, when it was unlocked, I discovered it full of women's clothes. There was everything from skirts to underwear and shoes. There were shelves full of porno flicks. What was going on here? Apparently, I dated a porn addict and a cross dresser. He eventually admitted that he was a cross dresser and he liked to prance around in those clothes in the privacy of his bedroom. Well he was a great guy otherwise. So I thought I could live with it. After some time I even thought it was funny and watched him wearing them. It looked kind of odd, a man with a beard and short hair, running around in high heels but then the next shocker. He told me that he wanted me to know everything about him and his past. I knew he was widowed, but he told me after his wife's death, he had sex with men. So buddy, you are bisexual. Time went on, then I had some car trouble, and Richard called his friend Ray to help him work on it. I knew he was one of the men he had sex with before. But I thought since he was with me now, it was over with. They were at my house, working on my car, while I was at work. One of the guys I worked with gave me a ride home, and as I got there, the car was not done but when I walked in my bedroom, my bed looked like someone had been in it. They had sex while I was at work. I was furious. When I questioned him, he didn't think there was anything wrong about that, since it was a man, he didn't consider it as cheating.

Time went on, his daughter's friends, gay or straight always seemed to have problems with their lives and it seemed like every time I was there, one of them was staying at the house. Some stayed with their kids, some with their gay or straight lovers. His excuse was "I am just trying to help them out". Then he started more and more suggesting that we should have a threesome sometime with another girl. Is he serious? Is he entering a midlife crisis, or is he going insane? There was that one girl named, Autumn. She was a friend of Cindy's who needed a place to stay with her three children. She was young and pretty. I'd seen the way Richard looked at her when she was visiting before. She had that slutty look and behavior, what a lot of man including Richard like. Well, she moved in with her children, Richard was helping someone out again. I usually stayed at his place on weekends when he was off work. He worked nightshift, during the week. Me, him, and some friends, would meet at a coffee shop in town, after I got off work and before he started his nightshift and had coffee.

Well, Autumn was always at his house now, very much to my dislike, I had a bad feeling about her. I noticed her hands would always shake. After I asked her about it, she told me that she was a, "recovering crystal meth head", yeah right. I knew enough about substance abuse, to know better. She had outstanding warrants. I don't even want to know for what.

January 2012 she finally moved out and in with her gay sister and her girlfriend. I was on my way home from the coffee shop one night, and a young girl, she was texting, took my right of way, slammed into my car and totaled it. She totaled my precious Mazda Miada convertible. I had wanted to make this car into an antique. It was eighteen years old and had only seventy thousand original miles on it. Now it was just a pile of metal. My knees went under the dashboard, I couldn't move, I felt blood running down my face and thought am I going to be ok? Somebody called an ambulance; I called Shiloh, from my cellular. She came right away. They cut my roof off what was left of my car, to get me out. They thought I either broke my neck or back. Meanwhile my daughter got in touch with Richard and by the time he got to the scene, they were just loading me on a stretcher and into the ambulance. Richard was already on his way to work but he called and explained the situation and his boss let him take a sick day so he could stay with me. I ended up with a broken nose, a concussion, both my knees had contusions. They were badly bruised and swollen, all the way to my ankles. I was not able to walk. He carried me home to his house. There was no way I could stay at home, on crutches, without electricity, and my dogs to take care of. I stayed there for three weeks. He would drive me every day to the house to feed the animals and spend some time with them until I was able to walk and to go back to work again.

During the time I stayed there, I got a good inside look at what all was going on in his house. No wonder he was always broke. His daughter was not working so he supported her and her son, and all those people going in and out living there at times and using him. One night, he told me, that Autumn borrowed over three hundred dollars from him. Oh boy, I knew, he wasn't going to see that money back and I was right. I ended up buying gas, groceries and cigarettes for him and his daughter then one night, he asked me, when my settlement from my insurance company would come in, that I owed him the hundred and fifty dollars he lost the night of my car wreck. He was hurting money wise, because Autumn didn't pay him back. What? I'm supposed to be your fiancé and you want to get paid for being by my side after my wreck, you got to be kidding.

Autumn finally got arrested for her outstanding warrants. I ran into her roommate at Walmart and she told me her and Autumn's sister were taking the three children to their Daddy's and she was not welcome there anymore. They found drugs in her room, and they were not going to bail her out of jail. I went to Richards's house and he had already gotten a call from Autumn asking him to bail her out of jail. He was just getting ready to leave the house, when I drove up. I told him if he bailed her out, I will leave right now and will never return. Well I was mad about it, because a few days ago Shiloh's German shepherd got lost and she, Andrew, me and all their friends spend every free minute looking for her, and put flyers out. When I asked Richard to help, he replied, "I don't have no gas money and the dog ain't stupid, she will find her way home." Well, how nice you want to bail that trailer trash out of jail, but you can't help what's supposed to be your family.

Well, he didn't go that night, but she kept on calling all day long the next day. His son who is a police officer, Cindy and I all told him that he needs to tell her no. He stopped answering her phone calls. Nobody from her family would bail her out either, so she stayed in jail until they finally let her go. I told Richard, that he needed to get his money back from her. He replied, "You know what, I got an idea, she can work it off. I make her have threesomes with us, she is really pretty, just what I wanted". I couldn't believe what I was hearing, I guess he noticed from the expression in my face that I was shocked, because he said, "Oh baby, I was just kidding". Yeah right. The next day, Saturday, I went to his house for the weekend. When I got there his daughter told me that Autumn moved in last night, because she didn't have no place to go. What!!! Get that bitch out of here. My fiancé was washing his truck, already showered, and dressed in his newest shirt and pants, usually by this time he is still in his pajamas and old house slippers. He came up to tell me hi, then the phone rings and it was her. When he got off the phone he told his daughter, "Cindy, Autumn just called she is coming home in a little bit, you need to go clean the kitchen, she said she wants everything spotless, when she gets home." What? I was sitting there waiting to see what is going to happen next. Cindy took off, she hated to clean. So, Richard runs in the kitchen, and started to clean. I am thinking oh wow just like a lovesick puppy. Then another call from her, he talks on the phone then goes to the freezer and takes some meat out, meat I bought. I asked him, "What is the meat for"? He replied, "Autumn told me to lay it out so when she comes back, she is cooking it for us." I have never been the jealous type, but this was too much for me. I started to pack my things, that I had over there and I even grabbed the meat. That bitch wouldn't eat food I bought, that's for sure. I asked him, "What made you think, I , your fiancé, owe you money for you taking care of me while I am sick, but she, who owes you money and is no relation, you don't want it back from her. But, in return you want to have sex with her.

Then I asked him for my house key back and gave him his and I was out the door. I went home, and finally turned my power on in the house, and started my life alone again. I talked to our friend Debby from the coffee shop about it, I wanted her opinion, wanted to know if I had overreacted, but she assured me that I'd done the right thing. Richard is still trying to get back together, but he does not realize that he was wrong. That girl didn't only destroy our relationship, but also Richard's neighbor's marriage.

I started hanging around with Todd, a guy I met at work a while back. We started to become good friends, he just got out of a bad relationship himself, and I guess we both where fed up with the opposite sex. He introduced me to his friends, and we all started to spend time together. A lot of people don't understand our relationship. They don't believe us when we tell them, that we are just very good friends.

Chapter 32

Time went by, and then my daughter called and asked me if she and Andrew could come to live with me for four to six weeks. They had lived in a camper on their property while they were trying to build a house. They decided to order a manufactured home, because, they didn't make any progress on the house. I was happy about it; I had the kids with me for a while.

Then the next shocker, a call from Marina my sister, my Step Dad died. This year has not been good to me. She asked me if I could come to the funeral. I told her I would. She needed some support from me, because my other four siblings had already started to turn into vultures, and she was stressed out. The day after the kids moved in, Shiloh drove me to the airport, my first flight ever in which, I would come without my daughter. She couldn't come with me, she had finals at school. I had a nice visit, with all my relatives, despite the sad reason, why I was there.

After two weeks, I went back home and my sister asked me for my bank account number and told me she would let me know when everything with his estate was cleared and then send me my share. Dad had signed over the farmhouse to her years ago. Her and her husband had done a lot of remodeling on this one hundred year old house and she took care of Dad, who lived there. He had also about five hundred thousand dollars worth of land that we needed to divide now between us other five kids. When I got home, my daughter told me, that she was pregnant. Ok, I was not ready to be a grandma yet, but I was happy for them. She told me it wasn't planed so they had to get used to it too. The four to six weeks turned into four months, but I was happy about it. I was not alone.

But this year had some more things in store for me. After two months my daughter lost the baby. Andrew had an accident on his four-wheeler and totaled it. My Great Dane got pregnant by Andrew's American Bulldog, my car broke down and I had to get a new car. They cut our hours at work. Then on top of it, I got thrown out of my Step Dad's will. After my loving Mother pointed out to her lawyer that my Step Dad only had given me his last name, but not legally adopted me, my vulture brother and his wife, demanded paperwork that proved, I never was legally adopted, so I didn't get a penny. Just at a time when I could use it the most.

Now here I am, Christmas 2012. The children got their house and moved out. I sold a litter of eleven adorable, "bull Dane", puppies. Now after fifty-two years, I am alone again. Every now and then, the fear of loneliness and desertion creeps up on me, tears want to get in my eyes and I think of all the abuse a lot of people had done to me. Then, I brush the tears away. After all, grandma told me not to cry and to be tough, right?

Life is full of dark nights. Is there any hope? I believe there is and that is why I'm still searching for the light!

www.ingramcontent.com/pod-product-compliance
Lightning Source LLC
Chambersburg PA
CBHW071335130626
46556CB00004B/1913